A New Jersey Love Story

Troy & Camilla

A Novel By

Myiesha

D1507888

Remember….
You haven't read 'til you've read
#Royalty
Check us out at
www.royaltypublishinghouse.com

Royalty drops #dopebooks

If you would like to join our team,
submit the first 3 -4 chapters of your
completed manuscript to
submissions@royaltypublishinghouse.com

© *2015*

Published by Royalty Publishing House

www.royaltypublishinghouse.com

Chapter 1

Camilla

"Hi, my name is Camilla. I'm here to see the owner, Troy for the waitressing position available," I said with a smile on my face, determined to make a great impression.

I needed this job and I was determined to win the owner over; not only with my million-dollar smile but with my looks as well. I stood 5'5", 140 pounds, brown skinned with a slender build. I was often compared to the actress Tiki Sumpter. I'm undoubtedly a beautiful girl.

At the age of 23, I was what people would call the typical girl next door. I'm smart and loved by everyone I come in contact with. I finished high school with a 4.0 GPA and was the valedictorian of my class. I was rewarded a full scholarship to Kean University. My first three years went by without a problem, until my mother was diagnosed with cancer and I had to stop going to help take care of her. Because I had taken a break from school, it caused me to lose my scholarship. When I enrolled for my last year, I had to pay out of pocket, which is why I'm here at Ladies Oasis interviewing for a job.

I sat at the bar waiting on the owner, Troy to come. The bartender said that he was on a conference call and would be down soon.

"Capri, let me get a double shot of Hennessy," I heard a male's voice say.

I looked over and locked eyes on this massive man. He was dark skinned, had to be about 6'5" and around 250 pounds of pure muscle. He was definitely eye candy and those dimples were so deep I could probably swim in them.

"Hello pretty lady," he said again.

I finally snapped out of my thought.

"Hey, what's up?" I spoke with a slight nervous stutter.

I don't know what it was about this man that made me nervous. I was never nervous around a person, that's why people loved me.

"Not much. Was wondering why a fine young lady like yourself was sitting here all alone so early in the day.

"I'm here interviewing for the waitress position, I was waiting on Mr. Troy now."

He laughed. "Mr. Troy, that's funny."

"What's so funny?"

"I've just never heard anyone refer to him as Mr. It sounds funny. I'm Supreme; I'm one of the performers here."

"I'm Camilla, nice to meet you," I extended my hand for him to shake. Instead, he took and kissed my hand, while keeping his eyes locked onto mine. The eye contact caused a chill down my spine. I don't know if it was from the feel of his lips or from those dark eyes he had. He was kind of scary.

He must have felt me shiver from the chill because once again, he started to laugh like he knew my dirty little secret. Seeing as though he was a dancer here, I'm sure it was part of his job make a bitch want to hop on his dick and start riding him in the middle of the stage.

"Don't worry sweetheart… that happens often."

I shyly laughed.

"Camilla," my name was called from behind me. I turned around to another beautiful man standing 6'1", about 200 pounds with the most beautiful Egyptian red complexion. He resembled the actor Laz Alonso.

What the fuck? I don't know how I'm going to manage to work in this place with all these fine ass men walking around here.

"Hi, yes, I'm Camilla," I said getting up from the bar stool.

Before leaving, I said bye to Supreme and walked away. Troy stared at me with those mesmerizing brown eyes and I couldn't do anything but blush. It was weird for him to be staring at me because he just seems way out of my league. He looked as if he was into the prim and proper girls, not around the way typical girls such as myself.

He waved his hand for me to follow him. We got to the elevator in the back of the club and he allowed me to walk in first. I felt him burning a hole through my ass. I didn't have one of those big ass video model booties, but I did have a little something going on. Thanks to squats, my booty sat up perfectly with no help from injections or implants. Some people said that I was too skinny to be carrying so much ass.

The elevator took us to the fourth floor of the club, which was his office. We walked into his office and I was taken aback by the way his office was decorated. It was decorated in black and white, with a white shag carpet throughout the office. The walls were painted an eggshell white, while everything else was black and glass. He had a large window behind his desk that allowed him to see out into the club. He motioned for me to have seat.

"So Miss Camilla, tell me a little about yourself."

Well it's not much about me. I'm 23 years old, a college student at Kean University, and I help take care of my mother because she was recently diagnosed with cancer. I have no kids and little work experience, which brings me to why I'm here today. I recently enrolled back in school for my last year and found out I lost my scholarship, so now I need to work to pay for my last year.

"Do you have a man, Miss Camilla?"

Why was this man concerned with me having a man or not?

He laughed. "I only ask this because we have had incidents where niggas didn't want their woman working in this kind of environment. This is a male strip club. There will be a lot of men walking around naked with big dicks. Are you comfortable with that, Miss Camilla?

"It's Camilla, please don't call me Miss. And to answer your first question, no I do not have a man and for you second question, yes, I am more than comfortable working in this environment. I'm here to do a job so there should be no reason why I'm uncomfortable."

He looked at me and licked his sexy lips while staring at me with those brown eyes. "I like you Camilla," he said while getting up from his desk and walking to a closet. When were you looking to start?"

"As soon as possible, I have tuition that needs to be paid."

"Stand up for me." I stood and he looked over me. He pulled out a few clothing items which I assumed was a uniform.

"You look like you could fit these. Here." He handed me three set of uniforms. I usually only give everyone two but being that I don't get a lot of girls that wear a size small, I have still plenty left.

"I got the job?" I asked overly excited.

"Yes, can you start tonight?"

"You damn right I can!"

"Good, see you tonight Camilla," he said with a flirtatious smile that made me blush.

I walked out of his office and immediately bumped into someone. I dropped my uniforms and bent down to pick them up. I looked up to a female who resembled the model Naomi Campbell.

"Oh, excuse me," I said.

"Watch where you're going next time," she said to me with an attitude, and stepped over me.

She was lucky I just got this job and wasn't ready to lose it, because I would have been on her ass like white on rice.

I shook my head and continued to pick up my uniforms. She walked straight into his office. I wondered who that uppity bitch was. I hope it wasn't his girl because he can do a lot better.

"Hey baby," she said walking into the office.

"I'm not your baby," I heard him say.

Yes! I said in my mind.

She went to kiss him but he moved his head. She reached down and grabbed his dick. And from the grip she had, I could tell he was working with a monster.

It was almost hard to tear my eyes away from his print but I did, and I continued to pick up my uniforms and made my way on to the elevator.

I made it back downstairs and there were two men on stage practicing what I assumed was a new routine. There were two women I assumed worked here on stage with them also. I sat and watched for a little while and made eye contact with the guy, Supreme I was speaking to earlier. It's like he had me in a trance because I couldn't pull my eyes away. He flipped the waitress upside down and pretended to eat her pussy in the air, while never breaking eye contact with me. He was a massive man. His body was oiled down; I'm surprised the girl didn't slip out of his arms because they were so greasy. The music stopped and he let the girl down. He winked, smiled at me and walked away.

"So how was it?" I heard Capri say from behind me.

"Huh?" I asked, finally turning my eyes away from the stage and towards her.

She was beautiful. I didn't notice until now, how much Troy and Capri resembled each other. She was a beautiful girl. She was what you would consider a red bone. She had high cheek bones, thick, pouty lips, and her body was bad. She had ass, hips and thighs for days. I noticed she had a tattoo on her wrist that said *Stash*.

"The interview with Troy… how was it?"

"Oh, it was great. I start tonight."

"That's good girl!! Welcome to the family mommas."

"I see this job comes with benefits," I said referring to the performance.

"Oh yea girl, they practice on the girls all the time."

"You ever let them practice on you?"

"Yeah right. For one, my cousin will blow a fucking fuse and two, my man would snatch me bald if he walked up in here one day and seen me up there."

We both started laughing. "I hear that. Who's your cousin?"

"Troy."

"Oh, okay. So who's that skinny chick that's in his office now?

"That's Keyonna's Beverly Hills ass. She thinks she's better than God, girl.

"Yea, I was about to shoot that hoe if she said something else smart to me."

"I don't know why my cousin still deals with that tramp. I think she fucking Supreme, but that isn't any of my business."

"Yo Capri," someone called her name.

"I guess I'll see you back here in a few hours," she said walking backward towards the kitchen.

"Yes you will babes," I said waving bye to her.

I looked up to the window to Troy's office. It was one of those windows that you can see out but the crowd couldn't see in.

I looked around admiring the rest of the place and walked out of my new place of employment.

Chapter 2

Troy

Keyonna walked into my office like she owned the shit. I mean, her father did help me make the money to open my club, but that doesn't mean I owe his or her stuck up ass anything. Yea, I fucked her on occasions. She was just a convenient fuck for the past two years.

Her rude ass walked straight over Camilla. I could see in Camilla's eyes that she was ready to pounce on that ass. Keyonna walked up to me and grabbed my already hard dick, from watching Camilla's ass as she walked out my office. I couldn't believe how much ass she was carrying to be so tiny. She couldn't weigh more than 130 pounds. I would be lying if I said I didn't feel some sort of attraction to her. I always had a thing for a slim chick with a nice ass.

I pulled out my dick.

Usually, I would just let her suck my dick but I wanted to punish that ass for being a bitch to Camilla. Keyonna strutted over to my desk, hiked her skirt up, and turned around with palms on the desk. I walked behind her, reached in my drawer and got a condom.

I kicked her right leg to spread them wider. Grabbing the back of her neck, I positioned my dick to her opening. Without warning, I slammed into her, knocking her forward, causing her to let out a scream. This bitch couldn't take this dick for shit, only down her throat.

"Oo Oo Oo, wait Troy, be easy, it hurts."

When she realized I wasn't letting up she tried to run. I had my dick so far in her that we were ass to pelvis. I just kept throwing the dick.

"What you mean be easy? You walked in here grabbing my dick like you owned it. You can't own it if you can't take it when you want it," I said to her. I started pumping faster. I closed my eyes and pictured Camilla being bent over instead of Keyonna. I felt myself about to nut. I opened my eyes pulled out, pulled the condom off, pushed Keyonna to her knees, jerked my dick and nutted all over her face.

I went into the bathroom, grabbed two washcloths and ran them under warm water.

I walked back into my office and tossed one of the washcloths to Keyonna for her to wipe off. I wiped myself off and looked up and saw Camilla talking to Capri. Her beautiful brown skin was radiant. She reminded me of an actress but I couldn't remember who. I completely zoned out not noticing Keyonna walking up to me.

"Why you staring at that basic bitch?" she asked with an attitude.

I ignored her and continued to wipe my dick off. Once I was done I walked over to my desk and sat down.

"Well if you're wondering why I'm here, it's because daddy asked me to drop this off to you," she said, handing me a yellow envelope. "He has another job for you."

I took the envelope from Keyonna and placed it in my desk. I picked up the folder with Camilla's information in it and was reading over all her information. I found out that she's majoring in business, and she was a very smart girl maintaining a 4.0 average in her first three years of college. I was very impressed with her stats. A woman with beauty and brains is a turn on for me.

"So you just going to sit here like I'm not here?"

"What's up Keyonna, what can I do for you."

"You can start by paying me some damn attention." I finally looked up and had to laugh a little bit because she still had some nut hanging off her chin.

"What's so damn funny Troy?"

"You have a little something on your chin," I said and looked back down to the papers.

She sucked her teeth and wiped her chin. "You didn't have to treat me like I'm some hood rat bitch. You need to show me some respect."

"You should have showed yourself some respect, you let me do it. Now why are you in my office right now Keyonna?"

"Remember, if it wasn't for my dad, you wouldn't be sitting in this fancy office."

I really hated when she threw that shit in my face. Yea, I do work for her father, and yes he is the reason why I was able to open up my business two years ago, but I'm the reason why it's still successful. He had nothing to do with that.

Outside of being the owner of my successful business, I was also a hitman. I kill for a living.

I was hired by this cat named Rome from out in Florida, to take out Stan. Stan got hip to it and paid me triple of what Rome was willing to pay me to leave Rome's fat ass sleeping with the fishes. Back then money was money; I didn't care who I had to kill to get the money. Since then, Stan has been hiring me as his personal gun.

I was always out on a job; therefore, I never had time to live life, which was the reason why I started fucking with Keyonna's whack ass. She was just a nut I needed every now and then, nothing serious. I've been fucking with her for two years, and she's walking around like she's my lady or some shit.

One day when I first started working for Stan, I went to his house go pick up my next job. Keyonna was waiting for me outside of his office. She pulled me to her room down the hall. Once I got in, she pulled my dick out and gave me the best deep throat ever. I don't know why I kept fucking with her. Head eventually led to me taking her virginity, and now I can't seem to get rid of her. Don't get me wrong, she was a pretty girl; she looked a little like Naomi Campbell, but she was just stuck up.

Once I made enough money, I opened my business and was now a part-time business owner and a part-time hitman. The envelope Keyonna handed me was for the next hit her father wanted me to do.

Chapter 3

Camilla

I walked in Ladies Oasis, nervous about starting my first shift. Besides the fact that it was my first day, I also had this small ass uniform on. The uniform fit me just right, but my ass cheeks were hanging out the shits. As Fetty Wap said, "She got cake for days." That was my favorite song to drop it to. But anyway, I knew this uniform would get me attention I didn't want.

"Hey, you must be Camilla. I'm Kitty; I'll be training you today." I recognized her as the girl on stage with Supreme earlier today.

"Well let's get this training started," I said with a lot of enthusiasm because I was eager to start working and collecting them tips.

"Where can I put my things?"

"Follow me," she said and we started walking. I couldn't help but notice she was a bad yellow chick, with an ass that almost could compete with mine. Not to miss the fact that she had a bubbly personality that just adds to her beauty.

After I got all my things in the locker, we walked back out to the main room.

"Ok, so you'll be working with me today in the cockpit."

"What's the cockpit?"

"It's the dancer's room, where they sit and chill until it's time to go on stage. You'll be working on the floor four days out the week with the ladies and the other day, you'll work the cockpit. Capri makes the drinks and we deliver them. Capri is the shit when it comes to working that bar; you have to taste her Tongue Twister."

"What's the Tongue Twister?"

"Some drink she makes that'll have you speaking in tongues, girl. Uhshammaladahada," she said speaking in tongues, causing me to laugh so hard I damn near pissed myself.

"You are nuts girl!"

"But anyway, almost everything here is electronically up to date, so this screen here is how we receive the drink orders. Each table has its own monitor where they can order their drinks and swipe their credit cards. If they want to pay cash, then we have to go to the table and collect."

"Okay, cool."

An hour had passed and I felt like I was catching on to everything Kitty was teaching me. The club was filling up with ladies ready to get felt up and slapped in the face with sweaty ding-a-lings.

I sat behind the bar helping Capri and was called by Kitty.

"Hey girl, we got orders. Let's go."

Capri prepared the orders and we walked the drinks to the back to the dancers.

I entered the room without looking up, and set the drinks on the table.

"Ok, who got the double shot of Henny?" With the drink in my hand, I looked up and my mouth dropped. It was like a sausage fest; dicks everywhere just swinging.

"I do," Supreme walked up to me, naked as the day he came out his momma cootie. I couldn't stop myself. I glanced down and I swear dude had to be half horse or some shit. I realized I was staring and managed to pry my eyes off his dick.

"Nice to see you again Camilla," Supreme said with a cocky smile. I was slightly embarrassed being caught staring.

"You too Supreme, here you go." I handed him his drink and everyone else, theirs. I never noticed that chick that I had seen in Troy's office sitting next to Supreme, until she got up and started walking toward me.

"Hi, we haven't formally met. I'm Keyonna," she said sticking her hand out like she was Queen Elizabeth or some shit. I grabbed a finger and shook it. I was still salty because of the way this bitch disrespected me earlier.

"Camilla," I said before grabbing the tray and leaving.

Remembering what Capri told me about Keyonna and Supreme messing around I had to agree. The two had to be fucking around. They were just too close and were comfortable.

I made my way out to the main room and the show had just started. There were two dancers on stage dressed as some fine chocolate fireman. The ladies were going crazy and dollars were flying everywhere.

I am really going to enjoy working here, I thought.

*****

It had been three weeks since I started working at Ladies Oasis, and had already gotten the hang of everything. I even started learning from Capri how to make drinks. I was moving around here like I had been working here for years. I would see Troy every now and then looking sexier than the day before. He would stop and have small conversation with me here and there, and then there was times when he would just wink, smile and keep it moving.

By the end of the night, I was exhausted. I kicked off my shoes at the bar and started rubbing my aching feet. I felt somebody take my foot out my hand. It was Supreme. He sat next to me and began giving me a foot massage while giving me the hungry eyes. You know if you come home with me I can make your whole body feel like this.

I gave a little laugh. I would never give him the chance to think he was going to destroy my insides with that pet iguana he's carrying between his legs.

"Uh, no thank you," I said taking my foot down. I got off the bar stool and went to help Capri and Kitty wash some of the dishes. I looked up and Supreme was still eyeing me like I was a piece of meat.

"Girl, don't worry about him, he tries to get with everybody." Kitty said

"Yea, some of them actually fall for his shit and he ends up leaving them crippled. That's why we always have openings for waitress." Capri added.

"Well, he won't be getting with this one, I tell you that much." I said.

"I hope not," I heard from behind me.

"Hey Troy," Capri and Kitty said in unison.

"Hey Troy," I said blushing a little because of the way he was looking at me.

"Stay away from that asshole, you hear me?" he said with authority. It actually caused my panties to get soaked.

"I would hate to see him run you off, beautiful. I might have to put a bullet in that nigga for fucking with you. How was your day?"

"It was pretty good. I'm exhausted and I have finals in the morning. But other than that I'm pretty good. How was yours?"

It was iight, you know… handling business like usual," he said picking up an ice cube and throwing it at Kitty's head.

"You's a big ass kid, you know that right," she said turning back around.

"Shut up," he said throwing another ice cube at her.

She then picked up the sponge and threw it at him and it hit his shit.

He got up and placed her in a headlock and started messing up her hair.

"Move Troy, God, with yo' yellow ass!" she pushed him and walked away. We all started laughing the way he fucked her hair up.

"That was wrong, you know that right?" I said laughing.

I turned around and continued to wash the dishes.

"You been gaining weight?" he asked.

"No, why?" I asked, self-consciously pulling on my shorts knowing they weren't going to go down no more.

"I might have to get you some bigger shorts." I turned around just in time to see him staring at my booty.

"See something you like?"

"I sure do," he said licking his lips.

"How are you getting home?" he asked.

"I'm going to take a cab back to my dorm."

"No, it's too late and you're too beautiful to be getting out of an ugly yellow cab."

I looked at him. "Well then I'll catch an Uber."

"Fuck outta here if you think I'm going to let you get in the car with some stranger. I'm taking you, go get your shoes."

"You're a stranger to me too. How I know you won't take me to your garage and lock me in your deep freezer or something?"

"Will y'all tell her I'm not a serial killer," he said to Capri and Kitty who seemed to move to the other side of the kitchen for some reason.

"Yea girl, he's not killer, just a little deranged," Capri said.

"See, now will you let me drive you?"

"Fine." I finished washing the last glass, dried my hands and went to pick up my shoes.

"Capri, make sure everyone is out and then lock up for me, baby girl."

"Ok," she said.

"Bye ladies," I said. They returned the "bye" with weird little smirks on their faces.

Troy grabbed my hand, leading me out the entrance of the club. As I was being pulled out by Troy, I felt like I was being watched. I turned and looked over to the stage and Supreme's creepy ass was watching us.

We walked to the garage and he clicked the arm to unlock the door. "Let's go, get in," he said trying to pull me.

"Hold up!" I pulled out my cell phone and took a picture of his license plate.

He laughed, "What was that for?"

"I'm sending it to my mother; just in case I don't make it tonight, she can give it to the cops and they'll catch ya serial killing ass."

He laughed, "Girl, come on."

I got in the car and it was beautiful. It had to be a new model all-black Range Rover. The inside was all-black leather. I was in love.

"Now where to?" he asked me, while turning on his navigation.

"Kean University in Union," I said.

"Oh, I know where that's at," he said and we pulled off.

Chapter 4

Camilla

We pulled up to the dorm within twenty minutes. "You can let me out here I will walk the rest of the way."

"What you mean? I ain't letting you walk over that dark ass bridge and through that dark ass field," he said after parking his car.

"It's okay; I do it all the time."

"Well, you won't do it this time," he said reaching over to the glove compartment and pulling out a gun.

"I doubt if you'll need that Troy," I said looking at him.

He looked at me like I was stupid.

"For one, I'm a little concerned that you didn't scream like most women do when they see a gun and two, this is Union New Jersey; it's filled with dumb niggas ready to do dumb nigga shit. I'm from here, ma. My mother doesn't live too far from here.

"Ok, let's go," I said getting out the car and walking ahead of him. I didn't think it was going to be this windy out. I had managed to put my sweats on in the car but my arms were still out and I had chill bumps. Troy took off his jacket and draped it over my shoulders.

"So why is such a beautiful young lady like you single?" he asked.

"I just don't have time to give at this point. With school and helping my mom and now working, a man is the furthest thing from my mind."

"Good," he said causing me to look at him.

"What you mean good?"

"I just mean it's good that you're focused."

"Uh huh. I see the way you be looking at me, I know you feeling the kid," I said joking around with him. He started laughing.

What was that wannabe gangsta thing you just did? Please don't do that whack shit ever again," he said causing me to laugh.

"So what's up with you and 'Black Barbie dressed in Bvlgari'?" I asked, rapping Lil' Kim's lyrics.

"Ah nothing, she's just somebody I hit every now and then. And her father and I do business together. He's the reason I have my club."

I appreciated his honesty. Another dude would have probably just lied about it.

"So my next question," he said, "is why didn't you react when you saw me pull out my gun?"

I stopped reached in my purse and pulled out my .9mm Ruger. "Troy, meet Minnie."

"Aww, look at it, it's so cute," he said picking on my little gun, causing me to laugh.

"Shut up nigga," I hit him. "It's cute but it'll do damage to a dumb nigga waiting to dumb nigga shit."

We got to the entrance and before going on my way, I made a detour to a small corner, moved a rock, started digging up dirt and put my gun inside the hole I dug.

"Why you doing that?"

"Because there are metal detectors when you walk in. If I'm caught with this on me, I can get expelled from school and I worked too hard to be expelled."

"I know," he said. "I was looking over your résumé and application, and it's pretty impressive. Beauty and brains…what is it that you wanna do when graduate?"

"I want to be an accountant; I'm pretty good with numbers. I also wanna open up my own daycare chain. It will be for hard-working single mothers that can't get assistance from the state. I feel like just because a single mom or dad has a good job and may seem like they can afford to pay daycare and put food on the table, doesn't mean their hard own money should have to all be spent on those things and at the end of the day, leave them flat broke. Yea, their kids are taken care of, but what about them, you know what I mean? The state goes by a parent's income, right? But they don't take into consideration the other bills that they have to pay.

My mom struggled when I was younger. She tried her hardest to get state assistance. They turned her down each and every time. Yea, my mom had a 9-5; yea, she was making more than 30,000 a year, but then she had to put clothes on my back, food in my mouth, pay six hundred dollars a month for child care, pay health insurance for the both of us, and buy me diapers. She worked in the city so she was commuting every day, so she had to pay to get back and forth from work. My dad always had excuses on why he couldn't help her. It was to a point where she just stopped asking him for anything.

It wasn't fair that people who didn't work as hard as she did was living better than her, eating better than us."

Troy reached over and wiped from something on my face.

I hadn't noticed that tears had started falling from my eyes, just remembering the tears she cried from the struggle she went through.

Before I knew it he reached over and kissed me. I wanted to pull away, but it was like his lips were magnets because I couldn't move. I just kissed him deeper. I don't know how long we were standing there, but I really didn't care. Finally, we broke away from the kiss.

"Uhh, I guess I'll see you at the club tomorrow," I said walking backwards.

"Yes, that you will," he said also walking backwards. "Goodnight Camilla."

Chapter 5

Troy

I walked back to my car with butterflies in my stomach. I don't know what came over me kissing Camilla, but she was just so beautiful with that sexy bottom lip and the fact that she had goals to help others, was a turn on; not to mention that her undercover thug ass carried heat. After hearing her open up to me the way she did, I knew I had to make her mine. I wanted her to have everything she desired, including her chain of daycares. I was going to make it my business to provide her with everything. She was going to be mine whether she liked it or not.

I got in the car and I had fifteen missed calls, all from Keyonna. What the fuck does this chick want? Seconds later, my phone rang again.

"Yo, why the fuck you blowing my phone up like that? Are you out of your mind?"

"I miss you boo," she said. "Come on over and let me show you what this mouth do."

"Keyonna, I ain't rocking with you like that no more, what we had is done."

"But Troy…" was all I heard before I hung up the phone.

If I wanted to start something new with Camilla, I knew I had to dead that bitch, Keyonna.

She called back to back the whole way to my house. I knew she wasn't going to let this go that easily.

I pulled into the garage at my mini mansion I had built a year ago. Although I was born and raised in Union, New Jersey, there was always something about Montclair that I loved.

I walked into my big empty house and just stood there. It would be nice to have a lady and some babies running around. I knew Camilla was going to be that lady.

I opened the envelope that was delivered to me today at the club. I pulled out some papers and attached to it was a picture of my next target. I never wanted names when it came to my targets. All I need was a picture, an address and places they frequently visited. I found out this nigga was from Harlem and lived on Lennox. I read that he was always in Paterson which wasn't too far from Montclair. His momma and baby mother lived in Brooklyn.

I put all the info away, and pulled out my cell phone.

"Yo Stash, what's good boy? I'm gonna come for big Shirley tomorrow morning. Have her big ass ready for me, aight? One," I said hanging up.

Big Shirley was the name of my AS50 sniper; I used her when my target was impossible to touch. This nigga was an easy target; I had another plan for big Shirley.

After getting off the phone with my nigga from day one, Stash, I went to take a shower. I reached for my jacket but realized I didn't have it on. I left it with Camilla.

After getting out the shower, I went and did my nightly ritual which was count the money in my safe. Although no one knew where I laid my head, I would still count my money and balance my checkbooks every night. I turned off the light to my office and went to bed. As I lay in bed, all I could think about was Camilla. I couldn't wait until I had her ass lying next to me.

*****

I woke up the next day feeling well rested and smiling. I walked to my closet looking for something to wear today.

I decided on my black True Religion jeans, a black Versace V-neck tee, and my red, black and white retro 11s, something simple.

I showered, got dressed and was out the door within an hour.

I pulled up to my grandmother's house half an hour late.

"Boy, you late as shit," was the first thing I heard when I walked through the door.

"I know Grandma; I had a business call right before I left out the door. My bad," I said before giving her blow-fish kisses on her cheeks.

"Ma not here yet?" I asked.

"Where yo' ass think you get yo' lateness from?" she asked, just before my mother came walking through the door.

"Hey Ma," we heard before even seeing her face.

"Girl, bring yo ass in here so we can eat. I swear you and your son gon' be late to y'all own funeral. If y'all black asses late to my funeral I'm haunting the shit outta y'all."

My g-ma was always going in on me and my momma, calling us black asses when we were both yellow as the sun. My grandmother was exactly what I called her— a g-ma. She was a gangsta grandma. Back in the day, my grandmother was one of the biggest drug dealers around. She was a queen pin. She was popped a few times and always managed to get out. She had one of the best lawyers around at the time, my aunt Viv, who was Capri's grandmother. The last time she was arrested, she was really facing some time but somehow the informant that was due to testify against her, turned up missing.

She begged me to never deal with drugs and I never have.

My mother on the other hand, was a straight diva. Before I started taking hits from Stan, my mother was a nurse. She hated her job but stuck with it to make sure I had everything I ever needed or wanted. That was something I was always grateful for. So to show my appreciation, I brought her, her own boutique, which she always wanted. It was a hair and nail salon on one side and it had a boutique on the other side where she sold clothing that she designed. It was the ultimate divas spot to get pampered. That's exactly what she named it: The Ultimate Diva.

We were seated around the table ready to eat. I went to reach for a piece of bacon and my hand was smacked by G-ma. "Ouch G-ma, why you hit me like that woman?"

"You know we say grace in this house. Now close your eyes and bow ya nappy ass head."

"Dear God, thank you for this meal you have so gracefully blessed us with. Thank you for watching over my Boo Boo and my baby girl. I thank you Lawd Jesus for allowing me to live as long as I have. Lawd, I just ask one favor please, bless my boo boo with a beautiful woman so he can give me some beautiful great grandbabies."

"Yes Lord," I heard my mother say a little too enthusiastically, causing me to peek from under one eye and look at her.

"In your name Lawd, Amen," we all said together.

"Really G-ma, did you have to include that in the prayer?"

"I sho as hell did. I want some great grandbabies running around here before I die."

"I guess I don't have to rush then; they say the ones that raise the most hell is gonna be the ones to live forever," I said joking around with my G-ma before taking a sip of my orange juice.

"Boy, shut up," she said smacking me in the back of the head, causing juice to fly out my mouth.

"So Ma, how's business going?"

"It's going pretty good baby. I just hired two masseuses, to make the ladies visit even better."

"That's good, Ma."

"I'm even thinking about expanding. The guy that owns the property next door is selling it. I wanna eventually have a play area with some experienced babysitters where the moms can leave their kids, while they get pampered and treated like the ultimate divas they are.

"That sounds excellent ma, just keep me up on that."

"That tramp, Kayla been asking about you. I had to send her nasty ass home one day. I swear if that girl didn't braid hair the way she did, I would have fired her. Coming into my professional establishment one day talking about how you banged her back out that night. How his Spider-Man was climbing her walls," my mom said mimicking Kayla. "Little nasty tramp."

I couldn't do anything but laugh. She has Kayla voice and movements down pat.

"Ain't shit funny, Troy; that girl ain't wrapped too tight, leave her alone.

"I did leave her alone Ma, it was only a one-time thing. Besides, I think I found someone. No," I corrected myself, "I know I found someone. She's beautiful, Ma. And she seemed so innocent until she pulled her gun out."

"What? I know she ain't pull no gun out on my Boo Boo," G-ma said getting up out her seat with the fork in her hand. I can only imagine how much damage my gangsta ass G-ma can do with a fork.

"No G-ma, not on me. Her name is Camilla, she waitresses at the club. I gave her a ride back to her dorm at Kean. I grabbed my gun, you know just for a little protection, and little mama pulled her piece out, basically showing me that she ain't need my protection. I'm gonna marry that girl," I said all cheesy.

"Alright Clyde, hold off on the marriage thing until I meet Bonnie," my mother said.

"*We* meet Bonnie," my G-ma added.

Chapter 6

Camilla

I had just finished my last exam and I was making my way across campus to my dorm so that I could get ready for work. I had my headphones on listening to Nicki Minaj's *Pink Print* album.

"Baby just get on your knees...I'll be back at 11 you just act like a peasant got a bow on my panties because my ass is present. Yeah it's gooder than Megan, you look good when you begging. I be laughing when you begging me to just put the head in. Let me sit on your face..."

What the hell? Someone had snatched my headphones out my ears.

I looked up and into the beautiful eyes of Troy. I started blushing. *What the hell is he doing here*, I asked myself.

"Hey, what are you doing here? Stalking a sista I see," I said making him laugh.

"Yea, you caught me," he said smiling. This nigga was too damn fine.

"What are you about to do?" he asked.

"Uh, going to get ready for work, I don't want my boss to fire me if I'm late."

"But it's only two, you don't have to be there until six."

"Well I have to take two buses.

"I'll give you a ride," he said.

I started to decline because I paid almost 200 for a bus pass for the month. I wanted to get as much use out of it as I could. Once I seen that he wasn't going to take no for an answer, that thought just immediately left my mind. "Alright, well I don't I have to be there until six, are you going to come back for me?"

"No, you're going to go wash ya dirty ass, get dressed, pack your uniform and go somewhere with me."

I loved a man in control, I thought.

"I ain't going nowhere with ya creepy, stalker ass," I said before turning around and heading to my dorm. He was right on my heels.

I felt him looking at my ass so I put an extra twist in my step.

*****

We got inside my dorm room and I went into my closet to find something to wear. He went and sat on my bed. He was looking so sexy in all black. I was happy I had my own dorm room. I was able to do whatever I want.

"Oh yea, here you go," I said handing him his jacket he let me wear last night. "Thanks again for making sure I was safe."

"No problem, ma. It seems like you had that covered," he said pointing to my purse. I laughed and walked to the bathroom to take a shower.

Twenty minutes later, I came out in just my towel. Troy was on the phone going off on somebody, so I just quietly went over to my dresser. I got my bra and panties out the drawer placed them on then took the towel off. I didn't care if he seen me in my underwear. I turned around and he was devouring me with his eyes. The way he was looking at me had me about ready to pounce.

"Keyonna, just lose all contact with me," he said before hanging up.

"Is everything okay?" I asked.

"Yea, this chick don't know how to take no for an answer. I let her know what she and I had was over, and that I found another pretty lady I wanted to get serious with. You trying to tease a nigga, ma?"

"No, I'm just so used to being by myself in here that it's just a habit coming out here naked. I'm shocked I remembered to put a towel on. I'm ready," I said, sliding on my 11s. He laughed.

"Ah shit, shawty matching my fly," he said pointing to our matching Jordans.

"That's right, but I look better."

"You right, I can't argue with that," he said.

I grabbed my bag with my uniform in it and we were out the door.

We were now sitting in his car and hearing him say he had someone else in mind had me slightly jealous.

"So who's this new girl you pursuing?"

"Just some cute ass brown-skinned college girl I been watching for a while now."

"Oh really?" I said.

"Yup," he looked at me with this cheesy ass grin. "She's spunky as hell and the best part is my new boo got a little gangsta in her. She carries this cute little Ruger in her purse… mad sexy."

"Oh really? And what makes you think she's feeling you?"

"I don't know but I'll find out. I'm putting the moves on her right now."

"Ha, ok, you're funny. Where we going anyway?"

"Somewhere fun, you'll appreciate it."

We pulled up to Bayonne Pistol Range. Troy got out and pulled this big ass suitcase from the back of the car. We got to the front where we were asked for our IDs.

"Are you guys renting guns or do you have your own?"

"We have our own, or unless you want to try a real gun other than that happy meal gun you carrying."

"Dude, don't be talking about Minnie like that. She'll do some damage. Yes, I would like to try that one," I said, pointing to a beautiful chromed .44 magnum Desert Eagle.

The guy set me up at the station with goggles, earphones and extra ammunition for the Desert Eagle. He also set me up with some ammunition for Minnie.

I've been to a gun range before, so my shot was on point. I didn't need practice at all, but this was my idea of fun. "Alright Sunshine, show me what you got." Troy said to me.

I placed the goggles and ear protectors on, loaded Minnie and fired, emptying the clip into the target. All my shots were landing straight down the middle, from the forehead down to his little paper dick.

I sat Minnie down and pick up the .44. This was a bit heavier than my gun so I had to get a handle on it. It didn't take long for me to get the hang of it. I hit all the kill spots. I heard clapping from behind me. I flipped my hair and dusted my shoulders off.

"Don't underestimate me, potna. Now let me see what you got."

"Oh no, no, no Sunshine, I play with big boy toys only," he lifted the suitcase. "Follow me."

I grabbed Minnie, placed her in my purse, waved for the attendant to come pick up that sexy gun I was just playing with, and followed Troy.

We ended up in a field I assumed was for long-range shooting. You couldn't see the target from where we were standing. Troy placed the suitcase in the dirt, took off his shirt and neatly placed it on ground.

"Sit," he said and I did just that. He opened his suitcase and I laid eyes on the biggest gun I have ever seen in my life.

Chapter 7

Troy

Camilla really impressed me with the way she handled that .44. I was also turned on by how good her shot was. And here I was bringing her here so she could practice; turns out she didn't need to. I might have to put Sunshine on my payroll.

I pulled out Big Shirley and watched how her eyes lit up. I'm almost convinced her fascination with guns was bigger than mine.

I set Big Shirley up and took a few shots hitting the target, which was about a mile away, hitting it dead center. I showed Camilla how to use big Shirley then let her take some shots herself. It was about 85 degrees outside; she took her shirt off and had on one of those bra things that the girls are wearing as shirts nowadays. She lay on the ground on her stomach like I was. I couldn't help noticing her toned back and how it dipped right before her ass. The sunlight beamed off her brown skin making her complexion look even more radiant. I watched as a drip of sweat ran down her back and was stuck in that dip. Her first few shots were off but after she got the hang of it, just like the Desert Eagle, my Sunshine was knocking off.

We stayed there for another hour before we were back sitting in my truck.

"So did you enjoy yourself?"

"Yes I did, I had so much fun. Big Shirley is the shit; I hope this ain't last time I get to play with her," she said with the fake sad face.

"Whenever you want, just let me know. We're here every weekend. We can make this our every weekend date, just the three of us."

"I would like that," she said before reaching over and kissing me softly on the lips.

"I can get use to that, Sunshine."

"Why do you keep calling me Sunshine?

"Because I think you're beautiful, like sunshine early in the morning. The way the sunlight beams on you causing your skin to give off a shine."

"Phahhaa, you're so full of shit Troy."

"I'm serious Sunshine, and you just hurt my feelings laughing at a nigga like that while he's all in his feelings."

"Aww, I'm sorry," she said kissing me again. "You know I can get use to these kisses," I said pulling back a little.

"Yea, me too," she said.

"So, where to?"

"Well it's a quarter to five, I gotta be to work at six, but I want to shower; I'm all hot, sweaty and dirty. You can drop me back off at my dorm and I'll just take the bus to work."

"Then you'll be late and then the boss might fire you."

"I have an idea," I said. "Do you trust me?"

"Trust you to do what?"

"Not be a psycho killer."

"You know I'm packing heat, and I know you ain't dumb."

"You ain't scaring me with that water gun," I said.

*****

We pulled up to my house. This was out of the norm for me because no one knew where I lived, just my momma and G-ma.

"Is this your home?" Camilla asked.

"Yup, all mine."

"It's beautiful!"

"Thanks, I drew up the blueprints myself," I told her.

"Wow, that's impressive," she said.

We walked inside and I gave her a tour of the house. She didn't know it yet, but soon this was going to be hers too.

"This is the guestroom; you can shower and dress in here and I'll be back in my room getting ready if you need anything."

"Okay."

I shut the door and made my way to my room.

I was out the shower and dressed within a half hour. I knocked on the door to the guestroom and Camilla told me to come in.

I opened the door to a beautiful sight of Camilla, bending over tying her shoes.

"Hey Sunshine, you ready?"

"Yup!" she bounced up and started gathering her things.

"Are you hungry? I was thinking about stopping at Chipotle," I asked.

"Ok that's cool."

After picking up our food, we made our way to the club.

Pulling up to the club, I spotted Keyonna's BMW parked by my spot.

Oh boy, I hope this chick don't make me kill her in this parking lot today.

I looked over at Camilla and she was finishing off her burrito bowl.

"Damn, ya greedy ass!"

"What? I was hungry, I haven't eaten all day. I was in class then you came and kidnapped me."

She was so cute.

We got out the car as Keyonna came walking up to me.

"Oh so you're an Uber driver by day now?"

"Thanks for today Troy, I really had fun," Camilla said walking up to me and hugging me, before smirking and walking towards Kitty and Capri who were standing outside when we pulled up.

"Anytime Sunshine."

She did that on purpose to piss Keyonna off. I couldn't help but laugh, because Keyonna turned green.

"Really Troy? That's the someone else you're trying to get serious with? Some little college waitress girl over me, a grown ass woman?

Girl, shut up, yo' ass ain't that much older than her. And at least she's working for hers and her daddy ain't buying her way through life.

"Troy, you ain't getting rid of me that easily!" Keyonna yelled before getting in her car and speeding off.

Chapter 8

Camilla

"Uh huh bitch, we see you," Kitty said. "Kicking it with the boss."

"Whatever, it's not even like that," I said smiling maybe a little too hard.

"Yea ok," Capri said. "Troy maybe my cousin but we're close like brother and sister. He's feeling you and whether you like it or not, you're going to be the lady on his arm. He called and asked how I felt about you. I told him I liked you, you were a nice girl, exactly what he needs in his life. Aunty Monica and G-ma will love you," Capri said.

"Hold up, you're moving a bit too fast, we haven't even established anything yet. We just had a fun day at the gun range and now we're at work."

"That's all y'all did?"

"Yup! Well no… he took me to his house to shower before work," I added.

"Ooooooooooo, yea bitch, we gonna be calling you Miss Boss Lady soon," Capri said before walking off.

I just shook my head.

"So that's how you rolling now?" I heard Supreme ask.

"What are you talking about?"

"I saw you getting out the car with the boss. That's what it is?"

"He just gave me a ride to work, although that's not any of your business."

"Well I'll let you ride, too, if you give me the chance."

"Bye Supreme." I walked off to the back to put my pocketbook up. I checked the mirror to make sure I was looking good. After I was secure with my look, I walked out the room and walked smack dead into Supreme.

"So I can't get that chance," he said grabbing my wrist.

"No Supreme, get off me."

"Aye Sun, I mean Camilla, can I talk to you?" Troy said. His timing couldn't be more perfect.

"Yea sure."

"Is everything okay here?" He must have noticed the tension between me and Supreme and how Supreme still had me by my wrist.

"Yea, everything's cool boss," Supreme said letting me go and walking off.

I walked toward Troy and he grabbed my hand and led me to the elevator. We rode up to his office.

"So what was that about?"

"He saw me getting out the car with you and had the nerve to ask if that's how I was doing it. I told him all you did was give me a ride and he gonna ask when can he give me a ride. I walked away and when I came from the locker room, he was there. That guy really creeps me out, Troy."

"Aye, don't worry about him, let me handle him, alright?"

"Ok," I said. I leaned in to hug him, but he lifted my face up and kissed me passionately. I returned his kiss with more passion. Before I knew it, I was being pushed on top of his desk. I started undoing his tie and unbuttoning his shirt, but he stopped me.

"Uh huh, not right now." He lifted up my uniform shirt, which was a crop top, and popped out my titties.

"Damn sunshine, you're surprising me more and more," he said, referring to my nipple piercings.

He put one in his mouth and it was all over. My juices started running like a faucet. That was my spot. I started moaning. It felt so good, especially since I hadn't had sex in a while.

I lifted one of my legs and placed my hands in my uniform shorts, and started rubbing on my clit. I needed to feel something at this moment. I was about to stick my two fingers inside my lady until my hand was snatched out of my shorts.

"Let me do that," he said pushing me back and taking my shorts off.

He moved me around to where his chair was, sat me back on the desk and pulled up his chair. He kissed the inside on my right thigh then the left. Seconds later, I felt his tongue start licking on my lady like it was a melting ice-cream cone. I threw my head back because it was too much for me to take. "Damn, you even taste like sunshine."

"Shhh, shhh," I said pushing his head back between my legs. I felt him beginning to nibble on my clit.

"Oh my god, Troy!" I shouted. I felt my body start to shake. I felt like I was about to explode. I tried to move but Troy gripped my thighs and I wasn't going anywhere. His tongue started to go in and out of my pussy. I couldn't hold it anymore. My body exploded, spilling all my sweet juice into Troy's mouth. He started slurping it up.

"Ahhh, Troy, stop, it tickles," I started laughing. I don't know what he was doing down there but he needed to stop cause I was about to kick him dead in his forehead.

"Aiight, I'll stop, but this not over. He walked away into his bathroom. I must have just come back to earth and realized I was spread out over his desk. Everything that was on his desk was now scattered around the desk on the floor.

I tried to get up but I was numb. It's been a long time since I'd had any kind of sexual play, beside my own hand playing down there.

"Lay down," Troy said, coming back into the room and pushing my body back down. He walked up to me with a washcloth. He started to wipe my lady down. I felt like I was a baby getting my diaper changed, the way he was wiping me. I started to laugh.

"Get off me, I can wipe myself," I said taking the washcloth out of his hand.

After I was done, I pulled my shorts up and my shirt down. I started picking up the things from Troy's desk and placing them on the desk.

"Come here, don't worry about that," he said.

I got up and walked to him. He grabbed my waist, pulled me in closer to him and kissed me. I pulled back.

"That was the bomb.com. You got a magic mouth, you know that?"

"Nah, I don't. That was my first time doing that. I never really trusted a female enough to put my mouth down there," he said touching my feisty kitty. She was ready to get it in but I wasn't going to put myself out there like that by raping him.

"So I took ya oral virginity?" I asked with a smile.

"Yup," he said smiling, showing them pearly whites.

"Aiight, go to work," he said, smacking me on my ass and pushing me toward the door. "Kitty and Capri probably looking for you."

"I'm sure their nosey asses know where I'm at," I said winking at him before leaving.

Minutes later I made it to the bar. They both were sitting there.

"Where you been skank?" Capri asked, with Kitty cosigning in the back.

"Around, why? Y'all were looking for me?"

"Around where? With ya lipstick smeared and ya hair looking like you were laying on it for the last hour."

"What?" I asked pulling out my compact mirror.

They were right. I pulled my lipstick out and reapplied it and brushed my hair back down.

I looked up. "You know what, MYOB bitches," I said walking away. I heard them laughing.

The night started and it was popping like always. I even found myself enjoying the show. After the show, the club turned into a party. Capri made us some of her Tongue Twisters.

Kitty was right, these shits were the bomb. I had one and that was enough to have me on the dance floor whining and twerking to Beyoncé's song "Standing on the Sun" remix. I even gave the bride to be a little lap dance. Her and her bridal party started throwing dollars at me. I was really enjoying myself. I looked on the dance floor and Capri and Kitty was also dancing with a bunch of woman who were there tonight.

By the end of the night, the club was cleared out and we were exhausted. I started wiping down the counter and I felt somebody push against me. I turned and it was Supreme. I slithered my way from in front of him and walked away. I have a feeling I might have to shoot this big nigga.

As I was walking, I walked straight into Troy. "Hey, you okay?" he asked.

"Yea, I'm good."

"No you're not; your nostrils are flare like a damn bull. Now tell me what's wrong."

"That nigga, Supreme is harassing me. I swear Troy, I'm gonna have to shoot that nigga in his neck he keep fucking with me," I said as I paced back and forth.

"Alright, give me a minute. Get your stuff ready so I can take you to your dorm."

"Alright."

Chapter 9

Troy

I walked back to the dancers' rooms in search for Supreme.

"Yo Supreme, let me holla at you for minute," I said waving him to step outside the room.

This nigga really had the nerve to take his time to come out.

"Yea, what's up?"

"What's up is that I'm fed up with the complaints about you harassing the women I hire. I've had more than one complaint. I'm gonna need you to clear out ya locker, I can't have you working in the club anymore."

"You fucking serious?" Supreme yelled with a vein sticking out of his neck.

"Yea my nigga, dead ass," I said stepping closer to him. He was a big nigga, but I wasn't scared of this steroid pumped up pussy.

"All of this over that bitch Camilla, right? Her pussy that good my nigga? I guess I really do need to get a taste of that."

Before I knew it I punched him in the mouth, causing this nigga to stumble. They said the bigger they are the harder they fall.

Once he gained his composure, he wiped his mouth, gave me a little smirk and walked off.

This ain't over Troy.

*****

I made it back to the bar to find Camilla sitting there with Kitty.

"Hey, you ready?"

"Yes, I am," she said. "Come on," she said, grabbing my hand and leading my out.

"Awww, don't they look so cute together," Kitty said. Camilla waved to them without even looking back. She must've been getting teased by them all day.

"Capri, baby girl, lock up for me."

We walked out of the club.

The ride to her dorm was a bit quiet. I parked in the parking lot and we got out.

"Are you okay?"

"Yea, I'm okay. What happened with homeboy?" she asked.

"I fired him. I was fed up with the complaints about him. He harassing you was the last straw."

"Oh, ok."

"So Sunshine, where in the hell did you learn to dance like that?"

"Omg, you saw me dancing?"

"Yup, I was watching ya hot ass out there. You looked like you were having fun. You're going to have to give me a private dance one day."

"You're such a peeper."

We made it to the dorms, got out, and headed to the entrance doors.

"Thanks," she said wrapping her arms around my neck, and I wrapped my arms around her waist.

"Anytime Sunshine."

"And thank you, too, magic mouth," she said kissing my lips.

"You got classes tomorrow?"

"No, I finished my finals today."

"Good, have breakfast with me."

"Ok, just call me in the morning so I can get up," she said walking backwards.

"How am I going to do that if I don't have your number?"

"Oh yea," she said running back to me. "Give me your phone."

I handed her my phone, and she put her number in it and handed it back to me.

"Ok, now you have it."

"Call me," she said throwing up the telephone sign with her two fingers, and disappeared through the doors.

I walked back to the car. I wasn't going home yet, I still had business to take care of.

I hopped in the car and drove to Belleville where I had my CL63 AMG blacked-out Mercedes parked in a community garage. I parked my Range in the lot and pulled out in my Mercedes.

I pulled out the envelope with the address to the places in Paterson where this cat from Harlem frequents. I found out he hung out over on Vreeland Avenue; I knew exactly where that was. I pulled up and spotted my target sitting on the hood of a car like some no-life nigga. He didn't look like much of threat, so I didn't know why Stan wanted him dead. An hour later, he hopped in his car and pulled off, getting on Route 80 back to New York. I followed close behind, but not too close where he would recognize he was being followed.

I noticed there was a green Expedition following me. I didn't know who it was following me but I needed to find out. I pulled up next to my target. My windows were tinted so I rolled my window down pulled out my AK and lit the car up with bullets. It was late so the lower level bridge was somewhat empty.

His car went swerving into the next lane, hitting another car before flipping over the rail and into the Hudson.

I sped off, now it's was time to see who the fuck was in that green truck following me.

I jumped on the FDR and the green truck was on my tail. I sped up a little but not too much; the truck rammed the back of my car.

Who the fuck could this be and how did they know it was me. They had to have been following me since before I changed cars.

I pushed the pedal to the floor and sped off through the streets of Harlem, losing them between Park Avenue and 125th Street. I knew they were looking for me so I circled back around pulling up behind the truck, pulled out my gun and shot out the back windows. I needed to see who was driving this truck. Whoever it was started firing back. They had on a hoodie so I couldn't make out a face. I just know this person was big and dark.

I wasn't too concerned about the bullets because I had my car custom made to be bulletproof. They continued to fire and I fell back. I didn't need the cops involved. I did make sure I copied the license plate number down.

I hopped back on the FDR. Once I was sure I wasn't being followed, I made my way back home.

I had a date in the morning with my future, and I didn't want to be late.

*****

"Good morning Sunshine, I'm outside whenever you're ready."

"Ok," she said and hung up the phone.

My phone started ringing again and it was Stan.

"Yo," I answered the phone.

"Well done, Troy. I'm satisfied and you will be satisfied when you check your account. One more thing Troy…why my baby girl walking around heartbroken?"

"I don't know, ask her. We never had anything serious. I asked her to fall back because my new girl wouldn't be okay with the little arrangement your daughter and I had. I haven't heard anything else from her since and I want to keep it that way."

"Troy, I like you, but when it comes to my baby girl I'll cut a nigga's eyes out for her."

"No Stan, you'll get me to cut a nigga's eyes out. You ain't about nothing Stan, but sitting on your ass and making money."

"Troy my boy, you don't want to make an enemy out of me."

"No, you're wrong Stan, you don't want an enemy out of me," I said hanging up the phone.

It was too early for this shit man.

"Hey you," Camilla said opening the door and getting in the car.

"Hey Sunshine," I replied, grabbing her hand and kissing the top of it. I was a little distracted, but I wanted to make the most out of my time with Camilla.

"You ready?"

"Yup! Where are we going, I'm starving?"

"None of your business… just sit back and relax, we'll be there in no time."

Chapter 10

Camilla

Minutes later, we pulled up to a house.

"You ready?" Troy asked.

"Ready for what?"

"To eat, you said you were starving. Let's go," he said getting out the car.

I got out and immediately asked, "Whose house is this?"

"My G-ma, you scared?"

"Uh, yea I am. Capri has been telling me about ya gangsta ass grandma." He laughed but I was serious.

"She's not that bad, I promise," he said grabbing my hand.

"Wait, how do I look?"

"Sexy as hell."

"Oh shit, really? Ya grandma gonna think I'm some kind of hoochie with this on," I said, referring to my tight peach maxi dress.

"Aye, you look perfect," he said before leaning in and kissing me on my lips. Ok, come on."

"Yo, yo, yo G-Ma, where you at?" Troy asked as walked in the house.

"Ya late nigga," his grandmother said. Aw shit, she sounds scary as hell.

We turned the corner to the kitchen where the voice was coming from, and there sat this little old woman and another beautiful woman who reminded me of Angela Basset.

"Dammit Boo Boo, why you ain't telling me you were bringing company," she said before running off to back.

"Hey baby," the woman who was sitting at the table said, as she got up and kissed Troy on cheek.

"Who is this lovely lady?" she asked.

"Ma, this is Camilla, Camilla, this is my mom. You can call her Ms. Moni."

"No she cannot, she can call me Ma," she said cutting Troy off and giving me a warming hug.

"Aiight, I'm back," the little old woman said, as she came back into the kitchen with some hair on the top of her head that wasn't there when she left.

I wanted to laugh so badly, but I didn't want to get my head knocked off by this old lady.

"Who this Boo Boo?" she asked.

"This is Camilla, this girl I was telling you about."

"Oh, my future granddaughter, huh," she said.

"Yup," Troy responded.

I looked at him and he flashed me that beautiful smile, and I started to squirm.

"Ooo, Monica, look," she said pointing to my squirming legs.

They both started laughing. Did I miss the joke?

"Don't worry baby, his granddaddy use to have that same effect on me when I was younger. That smile used to have my little kitty wet too."

Omg, this woman had no filter. I was slightly embarrassed.

"You can call me G-ma," she said leading me to the table.

The spread she had out was amazing. No way could this old lady have made all this food. We all sat down to eat. Ms. Monica said a prayer and I went in on the food. It's been a while since I had a home-cooked meal. I know they were looking at me like I was some kind of savage, but this food was on point. G-ma did her thing.

"Hungry dear?" G-ma asked.

"Yes, I am, and not to mention it's been a while since I had a home-cooked meal, living on campus and all," I replied.

"Well, now that you know where I live, you're welcomed here anytime. I'll fatten you right on up. Have them thighs matching that big ole thang you carrying behind you."

Troy started laughing and choking at the same time. I looked at him.

"That's what you get."

"Come on Sunshine, ya ass do kind of weigh more than your whole body."

"Forget you," I said mushing him in the head.

"Awww, I'm sorry Sunshine, come here," he said trying to pull me closer to him and reaching in for a kiss.

"Nah, get out of here punk," I said backing up. I couldn't resist anymore. Those lips were looking yummy, so I gave him a little peck and slipped a little tongue in. Usually I would have been uncomfortable being so affectionate with others around, but this time I wasn't; I was comfortable.

"Oooowee, that's right girl," G-ma said.

"So tell us a little about you Camilla."

"Well I'm 23, born and raised in Paterson. My mom was a single parent, and raised me all alone. She got me through high school, helped me apply to different colleges, and apply for scholarships because without them, I wouldn't have been able to afford to go. Luckily, an essay my mom helped me write got me awarded a full scholarship. I'm very thankful for all that she has done. A year ago she was diagnosed with breast cancer. The chemo took a toll on her body to a point where she couldn't take care of herself. Against her wishes, I withdrew myself from school so that I can help her out. By doing so I lost my scholarship. Now thanks to this kind and handsome gentleman here, I got a job and am able to pay my way through."

"That's wonderful, baby girl," Ms. Monica said reaching over and stroking my face.

After breakfast was done, I volunteered me and Troy to wash the dishes.

"I like her; she got my boy to wash a dish." I heard Ms. Monica say.

"I like your family. They're sweet. Your grandma is not as bad as Capri made her out to be."

"Oh, she's playing nice because you're new around here. Give her a minute."

"Ha!"

"You know what this means right?

"What?"

"You're mine now," Troy said.

"Oh really?"

"Yup," he said, drying his hands and grabbing me by the waist.

I wrapped my arms around his neck and we kissed each other like there was no tomorrow.

After breaking away, I told him, "Troy don't play me, I ain't got time for no games. Don't allow me to give you my heart and you don't do right by it. When I love, I love hard and I'm not afraid to bring Minnie out to eliminate anyone trying to interfere with my love.

My education is important to me; I worked too hard to get distracted now. Just respect that for this next year, school is my number one priority, ok?"

"Anything Sunshine," he said. "You're calling the shots baby, I'm just happy that I can call you mine."

"Oh, and I'm keeping my job," I said.

"That's fine, I'm just gonna have to find you some longer shorts. I don't need no niggas looking at what's mine, you feel me?

"Ok Boo Boo".

"Aight now, hold up, get your own name, that's mine," I heard G-ma say.

"Ok G-ma," I said laughing.

Once we were done with the dishes, we said our goodbyes and I had to promise to be back next weekend or I was gonna get my ass whipped. That old lady was a trip. I also promised Ma I would come and check out her shop.

"Where to, my lady?"

"Wherever you want, my man."

Chapter 11

Troy

To say I was a happy nigga was an understatement. I knew this woman was going to be mine that night I hired her. I looked over at her and smiled.

"What are you looking at you creep?" Camilla asked.

"You."

"Where are we going?"

"Just relax and stop asking questions," I replied.

A few minutes into the drive, Camilla had the itis and was on her way to dreamland. I noticed that green truck from the other night following me.

"What the fuck!!" I said out loud hitting the steering wheel.

"What's wrong?" Camilla jumped up.

"Listen Sunshine, there's some things you don't know about me that I had planned to tell you later on, but it seems like I might have to tell you sooner than later."

Before I could get another word out, the green truck came crashing into the back of my Range. I wasn't scared for me but scared for Camilla. This truck wasn't bulletproof like my Mercedes. If they started shooting, Camilla could get hit. I drove faster, weaving in and out of traffic.

"Who the fuck is that Troy?"

"I don't know Sunshine; the same truck followed me last night, too."

The truck slammed into us again.

"Oh hell nah."

Camilla pulled out her Ruger, rolled down the window and started popping off. My sunshine was mad gangsta. She was definitely my Bonnie.

Whoever was in that truck really wasn't expecting a bullet to come crashing into the windshield, shattering the whole window.

I was hoping to get a look at the bastard that's been after me, but whoever they were had a mask on.

She fired again and it hit him in the arm.

The truck started to slow down its pace and I sped up even more, leaving the truck in the wind.

Camilla came back in the window, placed her gun in her bag and started fixing her hair like she ain't just do some reckless ass shit.

"You good?"

"Am I good? I'm straight," I responded. "Ya crazy ass the one on a mission to die, are you good?"

"Damn straight."

"Ya momma should have gotten a check for ya psycho ass," I said and she laughed.

"Shut yo' ass up," she said punching me in the arm. "Now tell me what that was about."

She turned in her seat and placed her seat belt on.

"Oh shit!" she said, just before the truck was hit from the side, sending us flipping in the air. The car flipped a few more times before it landed back on its tires. I looked out into the road and it was cars pulled over on the side of the road. I could see another car was flipped over in the middle of the highway and someone helping them out of the car. I stepped out of my car and I instantly got dizzy. It seemed as if someone had grabbed me by my ankles and was spinning me around. I tried to walk but I stumbled a little. Some white guy came running to me asking if I was ok. I brushed him off and went to check on Camilla. She had a gash over her head and a few scrapes but other than that she seemed fine.

"You alright?" I asked her.

"Yea, I'm okay."

"Your head is bleeding," I said taking my white tee off and using it to control the bleeding on her head.

"You sure?" I asked double checking with her..

"Yea baby, I'm cool. I'm not as fragile as you may think I am."

We stayed there and waited for an ambulance to come. They finally arrived and we were taking to the hospital. Camilla had to get stitches for the cut on her head and a CT because she said she had a headache. Me on the other hand I didn't realize until I tried to help Camilla out of the truck that I had dislocated my shoulder. The nurses at the hospital popped it back in and ran a few test on me because I kept getting dizzy. Once all of our tests came back fine we were questioned by the police because one of the witnesses said they seen the other vehicle specifically target my vehicle. After I told them I was sure who it was that hit me we were discharged and on our way home.

On the way home, I noticed Camilla's hands shaking, so I grabbed her hand, kissed it and squeezed it tight. "Everything is cool Sunshine, alright?

"Yea, ok," she said. "Is this the kind of stuff I'm going to be dealing with by being with you?"

"Listen, I'm gonna be straight with you. I'm a hit man for a drug kingpin named Stan, Keyonna's father. He gives me information on people he needs eliminated. I handle it and collect money once the job has been done. I never leave witnesses because I'm never seen. I'm slick with my shit, so I wouldn't have any enemies. As far as what just happened, I have no idea who that is.

Last night after, I dropped you off, I went on a job. In the process of this job, that fucker in the truck showed up. I have no idea how they are tracking me but I'm pretty sure they followed me from your dorm. So you're going to be staying with me until I can find out who the hell that was."

I had a feeling she was going to put up a fight, but she didn't.

"I need to go get my things," she said.

"Don't worry about that shit; I'll buy you whatever you need."

"Ok." She said.

The taxi cab driver let us out in front of the house.
I opened the house door for her to go in first.

She kicked off her shoes and pulled off her dress.

"Do you mind if I shower?" She turned to me with her hands on her hips and her perky breasts sitting up and her nipple rings trying to rip through her bra.

I sat my keys and my phone down on the counter and walked up to her.

I picked her up by her waist and stuck my tongue all the way down her throat. She wrapped her arms around my neck.

I walked her over to the wall, placing her back against it. I used the wall the slide her up and placed her legs on my shoulder. I moved her panties to the side with my teeth. She was so wet and it tasted so sweet. I started eating her pussy so hard using teeth, tongue and lips. I started fucking her with my tongue; I think I found my new addiction.

Her pussy had me moaning like a little bitch. I felt her body start to shake, her moaning getting louder.

"Troy, I'm cumming baby," and before I knew it, she started squirting and I licked every drop of it up. Her body went limp.

I slowly slid her down to her feet.

She kissed me and turned me around so that my back was against the wall. She took off my shirt and started kissing on my chest, as she slid her tongue down my body until she reached my pants. She dropped down in a squatting position.

I was ready for Sunshine to show me if she had skills or not.

She pulled my dick out my pants and her eyes lit up. I expected her to be afraid but she didn't seem scared of my size at all. She looked up at me, grabbed my dick and started licking it like she was licking on an ice pop. She licked up the vein and back down. She placed her mouth over the head and started bobbing up and down taking, me all the way to the back of her throat, damn near swallowing my shit. I thought I would never find anyone to suck me like Keyonna, but I was wrong. My sunshine was better. She spat on it and used her hand to start jerking me. She lifted my shaft and started giving my balls some attention, as she sucked one in her mouth and popped it back out. She grabbed the other and put both in her mouth at the same time, while jerking my dick.

She was an undercover freak and I loved every minute of it. She came back up and deep throated me until I was on the verge of squirming like a little bitch.

"Damn Sunshine, where you learn that from?"

"This pleasure party I hosted," she said with a smile. She tried to go back down but I grabbed her up and walked her upstairs to my bedroom.

I threw her wild ass on the bed, and removed her panties and bra. I climbed between her legs and slowly guided myself into her wetness. Her shit was on the money. It was so tight her pussy could have sucked the skin off my dick if I pulled it out too fast.

I started pounding into her, giving combinations of long and short strokes. She pushed me and turned around on all fours.

"That's how you want it Sunshine?"

"Yes, daddy," she moaned.

"Umm... ok." I grabbed her hips and started pounding her little ass out.

My baby was taking this entire dick. I was going in; it felt like I had just ran a marathon. Sunshine was still holding in there.

Her body started to shake and so did mine. I was trying to hold out but I couldn't. I came all in her.

Chapter 12

Camilla

I woke up the next morning after getting my brains sexed out, feeling hella relaxed. My head was still killing me. I looked at the clock and it was ten in the morning. I didn't realized how long I had slept. I turned over and Troy wasn't in the bed with me. Yesterday was very eventful, I thought. I met Troy's crazy ass family, Troy made me his lady and I was almost killed on the road today. I got up and decided to go in the bathroom to go wash. His bathroom was beautiful and huge. My dorm room could fit in here twice. Everything was snow white and the accessories were glass. Not that fake ass plexiglass you get from the dollar store, but real glass. It had stairs that lead to a Jacuzzi in the middle of the bathroom. There was a vanity that was empty with a plush stool pushed under it. There was a step in shower with the massaging showerhead. I walked over to a closet and my nosey ass opened it. It was stocked with towels and washcloths, Dove White body wash, Dove deodorant, Vaseline Cocoa Butter lotion—everything a bathroom needs.

I got into the shower and used his Dove White shower gel to wash with. I rinsed off, grabbed a towel and wrapped myself. I walked out in search of Troy because I had nothing to wear. I had to be to work in an hour and I forgot to grab my uniform. I walked throughout the house familiarizing myself with the place. There were two rooms set up, I assumed for guests, both with bathrooms, then there was an empty room, I wondered why this room was empty. I walked further to the back of the house and there was another door in the corner that led to an outside patio that was fully furnished. It had a grill, a bar and a set of stairs that led down to the first level of the house, and then more stairs that led to an indoor pool in the basement. I had to say he really outdid himself when he drew up the blueprints to this house. I walked back up the stairs to the patio and just relaxed until Troy decided to show his face, because I couldn't find him anywhere.

It was about 90 degrees outside, so I just sat outside in my towel listening to the music from my phone. I was listening to K Michelle "Hard To Do." That was my bitch when I felt like being ratchet.

"What you gonna do when I put this pretty thing on you. I usually don't this but I'll do it for you oh. Baby cause missing you is way too hard to do, I'd rather be fucking you, do mind if I give you love."

I put my hand inside my purse because I felt a shadow standing in front of me. I opened my eyes and it was Troy looking so sexy in just a wife beater with his tats showing, a pair of khaki shorts and a fresh pair of all-white Air Forces. He had bags from Express and Victoria's Secret in his hand. I pulled my earphones out and smile up at him.

"Hey sexy."

"Hey Sunshine, I see you found ya way around the house."

"Yup, I think I found my second favorite place in the house."

"Oh really, what's the first?"

"Under you," I said reaching over, undoing his belt buckle and unzipping his shorts.

"You know I gotta be at the club in like an hour, right?"

"This won't be long baby, I promise. Besides, you're the boss, what you going to do fire yourself?" I said before I took his little man in my mouth and gave my man the best head he'd ever gotten.

I kept sucking until I felt him start to shake.

"Oh shit Sunshine, I'm about to cum," he said trying to push my head, but I wasn't moving. I was about to mark my territory; this was my dick and another bitch better not try me.

I swallowed every drop he had to give.

"Damn Sunshine," he said falling back on the chair next to me.

"So what's in the bag?"

"That's for you," he said weakly pointing to the bags.

I laughed at him because I had literally sucked all the life out of him.

I opened the Victoria's Secret bags and was that there was a bunch of pantie and bra sets. I know he had to pay about fifty dollars apiece for each set. Inside the Express bags were a couple outfits.

"How did you know my size?"

"I guessed," he said, sleepily. "I'll take you tomorrow to get some more clothes; I figured you needed something for now."

"You figured right," I said taking off the towel and placing the underwear on. He had good taste, I'll give him that.

I put on the valor short set he had in a Bebe bag. It fit perfectly.

"You're the bomb baby; you know that," I said to him.

"I know, ma," he said smacking me on the ass.

*****

We pulled up to the club about an hour later. We got out the car and I walked over to him and grabbed his hand, as we walked into the club.

"Hey y'all," Capri said.

"Hey boo," I said kissing Troy on the lips before I walked over to the bar and jumped on top of it.

"Uh huh trick, you may be doing the boss but you ain't about to be plopping all that ass on my bar?" Capri asked

"Aye, leave my baby alone, aight?"

"Boy bye!"

"What's going on sis? How are things around here?" Troy asked.

"They good, like always."

"That's what's up, that's why I pay you the big bucks."

"Baby, come upstairs when you're done."

"Alright," I said with a smile.

"What the hell happened to your head chick?" Capri asked.

"Car Accident" I said

"So, you heard Supreme got fired?"

"Yup, sho' did! That's what his creepy ass gets."

"Maybe we can start keeping employees now."

"Supreme has been harassing bitches away from this club for a long ass time. You come along and he loses his job," Kitty said taking me and Capri by surprise.

"Since when you became team Supreme?"

"Whatever," she walked away from us.

"Uhh, what the hell was that about?" I asked pointing.

"I don't even know," Capri said.

Shaking my head, "I'll catch you in a few," I said, jumping off the bar. "I need to go get a uniform from Troy."

"Okay," Capri replied.

I walked out the elevator into Troy's office.

Where the hell did this bitch come from? I thought to myself. I could have sworn he told her to stay away.

"Hey baby."

"Hey Sunshine," he said.

I reached over, kissed him and sat on his desk with my back toward that hoe like she wasn't even sitting there.

"Excuse me, don't you see us talking?"

"No I don't, I see you sitting there and my man sitting over here undressing me with his eyes," I said not even giving her eye contact. "Besides, didn't he ask you not to come back here?" I asked now getting up and turning to her.

"He ain't mean it, did you Troy?"

"Yes the hell he did bitch; now kick rocks hoe."

"I ain't going nowhere until he tells me to go," she said getting up and walking toward me.

"You heard my lady, she told you to kick rocks now go and do just that."

"Really Troy, you let this little bitch call the shots now?"

I reached back and punched that bitch dead in her mouth. She fell flat on her ass.

"Call me another bitch."

She charged to me full speed and I moved out the way letting her dumb ass run head first into the window.

I grabbed her by her hair and she swung around and hit me in my mouth. I felt my lip bust. I wrapped my hands with her 22-inch weave and started busting the bitch's face wide open.

She started screaming for Troy to help her. I started stomping the wind out of her body. "Don't you ever let my man name fly out ya mouth, bitch."

I let her go and she fell to the ground limp. I walked into the bathroom to clean myself up.

"She really split my shit, ole plastic bitch."

I took the clothes I had on, off because they had blood on them.

I walked out of the bathroom and the bitch was gone. I walked over to the closet where the uniforms were at and took one out. Troy was still sitting at his desk where I left him.

I put the uniform on and walked over to him and kissed him on the lips.

"See you later, baby."

"Alright Layla Ali."

"Shut up, she better be happy I ain't have my purse," I smiled at him and walked out his office.

Chapter 13

Troy

Watching Camilla beat the shit out of Keyonna had my dick rock hard. My baby was willing to get down and dirty for me like I was willing to do for her ass.

Keyonna was no match for my Sunshine in the bedroom or with the hands.

Before Sunshine walked in, Keyonna was telling me about her father having a hit out on me and how she can make it all go away if I agreed to be with her. Bitch done lost her mind.

Her father didn't scare me, nobody did at that. I was the best hitman alive. His fat ass wanna put hits out, I got something for his ass. This shit was comical to me.

I picked up my phone and called Stash. We haven't kicked it in a minute. Capri ass done wifed my nigga and barely came out the house.

Stash and I go way back. We met in high school.

I was walking in the school yard one day and I noticed a bunch of people crowding around something. I wanted to walk away but something was pulling toward the commotion. I pushed my way through and noticed three boys I recognized from my hood, jumping some boney, malnourished looking kid. They were kicking his ass bad.

Although I was from the same hood as the other three boys, I was nothing like them. I wasn't well liked but everyone knew not to fuck with me. I had a fascination for guns. At 15, my mother bought me my first gun and every birthday after I received a new one. She would never buy me the bullets.

I stepped in and defended this kid. I pulled out my .9mm glock and pulled one of the kids in a headlock and placed the gun to his head. I had no bullets in the gun but they didn't need to know that. The other two boys walked off with their hands in the air. I released their friend and they all ran off.

I picked the kid up and helped him pick up his things that were scattered around.

"I'm Jorel, good looking."

"I'm Troy. Why them niggas fucking with you anyway?"

We finished picking up his things and started walking.

"Oh, they looking for this," he said taking off his shoe and pulling the sole open and pulling out money.

"Where the hell you get that from?"

"I stole it out one of their book bags," he replied. I'm known around here as Stash because I can steal anything and you'll never know it until it's too late. I'll steal your shirt off your back and you'll never know until you get home and get ready to undressed."

"You think you that good, huh?"

"I know I'm that good. Where did you get that gat from?"

"My mom brought it for me. I have a collection."

"Word? You think I can see it one day?"

"Sure."

Since that day we've been tight like a fresh weave. You'll never see me without him or him without me. The longest we were ever apart was when he joined the army when he turned 18. He became a firearms specialist and then was recruited to Black Ops.

He was my connect to the specialized firearms no one else could have ever gotten their hands on.

Stash wasn't that wimpy kid that I rescued in the park back then. This nigga was two times bigger than me. He stood about 6'4" and 310 pounds of pure muscle.

When he came back from his deployment three years ago, I hooked him up with my cousin, Capri, my aunt Viv's granddaughter. They have been rocking ever since.

"My hitta, my hitta!" he answered the phone.

"What's good?"

"Shit nigga, get yo' ass out of that basement for a while and come kick it with me. I got someone I want you to meet."

"Who, ya new shorty? What's her name? Camilla?"

"Haha, nobody but ya big ass mouth girl done told you, huh?"

"You know she did, and don't talk about my baby like that, iight."

"Nigga shut up and find ya balls. Capri probably has them in her pocketbook. Look, come meet me at the club, I got some business I wanna talk to you about.

"Iight, I'll be there," he said and we hung up.

I got up and looked out the window. The club was packed. Onyx and Luna was on the stage giving one hell of a show. The ground was covered in bills. They were out main attraction. Them two always brought in the bucks. They gonna need a broom to get all that money up.

I looked around for my boo and she was standing by the bar waiting for Capri to finish making the drinks. Looking at her made my heart jump. I couldn't wait to get her home; I wanted to make love to her in every position. I know it's too early to be considering love, but I've never felt anything so strong in my life. I'm gonna marry that girl. Little did she know she didn't have to work anymore, but I could tell she liked the job. If she wanted to continue working here it was fine with me, but I was gonna start making her ass put some jeans on. Now that she was mine, I didn't need other niggas looking at what belongs to me. I noticed that nigga, Luna staring too hard; I didn't want to fire his ass like I did Supreme, but I would.

I sat down at my desk to finish of some paperwork. Fifteen minutes into completing these business documents, someone was ringing the elevator bell. I looked at the screen and it was Stash. I buzzed him up.

"My Hitta!"

"My Nigga!"

"I missed you baby, you need to get out more."

"Yea, yea you know where I live, you're always welcomed. You got a key, use that shit sometimes. If you just happen to walk in and hear screams, don't be alarmed; it's just me tearing it up, nah mean," he said reaching for some dap.

"Nah nigga, that's my cousin."

"Whatever hater."

"I ain't got shit to hate on, my baby right downstairs."

"Oh yea, come show me this Camilla that got you looking like the heart-eyed emoji."

"Shut up nigga, she right there," I said pointing.

"The little brown skin by the bar?"

"Yup, that's my Sunshine."

"Sunshine? And you telling me to get my balls back from Capri?"

"How long y'all been kicking it?"

"About a month now and she's it man. Shorty bust guns like a nigga, no hesitation. And she puts it down on a nigga in the bedroom too."

"Word?"

"Hell yea, that's what I asked you to come here for. Last night I was followed while I was taking care of a job Stan put me on. I noticed some nigga following me in a green Expedition. I handled the job and next thing I know I'm being chased through fucking Harlem. I snuck up behind whoever it was and blew out the windows and then sped off.

Earlier today we leaving G-ma house, and the same truck pulls up behind me again. Next thing I know, Camilla's gangsta ass pulls out her burner and starts giving it to the niggas with no worries of taking one to the dome. I need to find out who the fuck this is and off they ass. I can't have this happen again."

"Did you get a plate number?"

"Nah."

"I got a hookup down at the PD; I can probably get them to pull up everyone that drives a green Expedition in Jersey and New York."

"Aight, good looking homie."

Boom!

"What the fuck?" both Stash and I said at the same time. It was like a bomb had just gone off.

I looked out the window into the club and everything seemed fine. However, I also noticed there were customers scattering to get out of the door. It was like a stampede of women. I watched as Camilla jumped up on the bar so that she wouldn't get trampled.

I pulled up the cameras and I saw that my garage was on fire.

I scanned through the camera and seen the green truck driving off. I tried to catch a glimpse of the plates, but they had some kind of protective shield over them.

My security team was already on their way outside.

I went down to the floor and walked over to Camilla to make sure she was good.

"You good baby girl?"

"Yes babe, I'm fine. What was that?"

"Someone set the garage on fire."

"Who would do that?"

"I don't know but I'm gonna find out," I replied. "Oh Sunshine, this is my boy Stash. Stash, this is my beautiful Sunshine."

"Nice to meet you, ma."

"You too."

I heard the fire truck sirens so I grabbed her hand and we all walked out to the garage.

When we got out there the whole shit was burned down. Thank God I parked in the parking lot today. God must've really been looking out for me.

"Look Sunshine, I'm gonna be here for a minute. Here are your keys for the house and I'll text you the alarm code. Take my car and wait for me at the house," I said handing her the keys to the Mercedes.

"Alright babe," she reached over and kissed me. "See you when you get home. Be ready for some extra nookie nookie when you get home," she said winking at me, making my silly ass blush. I smacked her on the ass.

"I'll call you in the morning Capri, so we can go shopping," she said before walking off.

I don't know what it is about this girl that's turning me into a bitch.

"Nigga is you blushing?" Stash said to me.

I ignored his and Capri's little smirks they had on their faces.

Chapter 14

Camilla

On the way driving to Troy's house, I felt like I was being followed. I kept checking the rearview mirror but none of the cars looked suspicious.

I pulled into the driveway and sat there trying to figure out how to get the garage open. I found the button and the door slid up.

I pulled in and noticed there was a car with a blue tarp on it. This must be a new car cause that wasn't there when we left.

I was tempted to go look at it but I decided against it.

I walked in the house, left my purse in the kitchen and went to take a shower. I turned on the Jacuzzi to warm it up. Once I was done washing, I hopped in the massive Jacuzzi and just let my body soak.

I ended up dozing off and was awakened by the doorbell ringing. I jumped out, grabbed my robe and ran down the stairs.

I looked out the peephole and couldn't see anything. I looked out the glass windows on the side of the doors still didn't see anything. I placed the chain on the door, turned off the alarm and cracked the door. I looked out and into the face of the last person I expected to see.

*****

Green Truck

That nigga Troy though he had seen the last of me, but he was sadly mistaken. For him to think he was gonna punch me in my shit and get away with it, this nigga had to be a fool.

Once Keyonna told me Troy and Camilla were together now, I was ready to fuck his whole life up.

After I set the garage on fire, I expected him to get in his truck and be out. I never expected him to send Camilla to his crib alone. I had set a bomb in the car to blow the shit up on the highway, but I had a better plan now. I was gonna get what I've been wanting for a few weeks now.

Clown motherfucka!

****

Camilla

"What are you doing here Supreme? How did you know where Troy lived?"

"I didn't, I followed you from the club. Open the door so we can talk beautiful."

"No Supreme, you need to get going," I said, attempting to shut the door, but he placed his foot in between the door.

I pushed hard trying to hurt him so he could move his foot. I continued to push until he moved his foot and it closed. I took a sigh of relief until I hard glass shattering.

I turned around and he had thrown a chair through the window on the side of the door.

He climbed through the broken glass and I took off up the stairs. I made it up the first five stairs before I felt my hair being pulled out from my scalp, and I was being pulled down the stairs. I was thrown into the wall, hitting my head so hard I was seeing stars.

"Supreme what do you want?"

"What I always wanted and you keep playing."

"Please don't do this Supreme," I said before I picked up the vase that was sitting on the table next to me, and smashed it into his face causing him to let my neck go.

I ran up the stairs taking two at a time, until I reached the top and ran into the bathroom.

"Shit, shit, shit!!" I yelled, damning myself.

Why did I run in here instead of the kitchen where my cell phone and my gun was. I heard the doorknob jiggle

"Supreme, just leave!" I yelled from behind the bathroom door.

"Bitch, open this door or I'm kicking the shit down. I'm about to get what I came here for!"

I searched through the bathroom for a weapon, something to protect myself with.

Boom... Boom... Boom

I hurried to the closet to find something, anything, but there was nothing. If only I had my gun.

Boom... Boom... Boom... The door went flying off the hinges and across the bathroom floor.

Supreme came walking into the bathroom with a sinister smile across his face. I ran towards the sink and reached for the glass soap dish. I slammed it against the sink and it shattered. I searched for the biggest piece I could find. Supreme came running towards me at full speed.

I quickly turned around and slammed the glass into his chest as hard as I could.

He let me go and a sigh of relief left my body. I thought I had actually done something. He looked down at his chest and back at me. Never breaking eye contact, he pulled the glass out of his chest and threw it on the floor.

"Oh shit!!

He picked me up and threw me into the vanity mirror. I hit the floor with so much force that I felt a few ribs crack. Supreme stood over me smirking. Before I knew it, his size 12 boot came crashing into my face, immediately cracking my jaw. He continued to kick me.

He reached down and pulled my robe off exposing my naked body. He looked down at me like I was three-course meal. I could literally see the slob forming in his mouth. He got down on his knees and started unbuttoning his pants. I tried to move to get away, but I couldn't. I was in so much pain.

He reached down and grabbed my breasts and started playing with my nipples. I wanted to cry but I couldn't. He placed my nipple in his mouth and started to suck and bite. Normally I would be turned on but this wasn't the time. He bit down as hard as he could, as I screamed out in pain.

He came up and he had blood dripping from his mouth. I spit in his face.

"Oh bitch, it's on now."

He reached in his pants and pulled out his dick.

"You think you tough, huh?" he said before spitting in his hand, rubbing it on his dick and shoving the entire thing inside of me.

It felt like a baby was trying to climb inside of me. I didn't want to show weakness although it hurt like hell. I started to fight back. I punched and clawed at his face. He grabbed both my arms and lifted them above my head. He started to ram himself in and out of me and each time I felt like I was being ripped. He grabbed my other breast and started to suck and bite. I felt so disgusted.

All I wanted was Troy, all I needed was Troy. I didn't realize I called Troy's name.

"Oh, you thinking about that bitch? I got something for that ass."

He turned me around and placed his face in the crack of my ass and started licking. He then spit in it.

He grabbed his dick and bit by bit he slid in my ass.

I momentarily blacked out from all the pain. I felt something leaking down my legs.

Ten minutes later, I was being turned back around. He started jerking himself and then crawled to my face.

"Hold this," he said before nutting all over my face.

He got up grabbed my robe and clean his dick off with it and pulled his pants up. I never noticed he had a gun until he pulled it out. "It was you who shot at me the other night, right?"

"Fuck you bitch ass nigga."

"No, that's what I just did to you and it was everything I imagined. Tell Troy he fucked with the wrong one."

I heard a shot before feeling burning all over my body, and then everything went black.

Chapter 15

Troy

After getting all the insurance papers and police reports squared away, I asked Stash to give me a ride home. He sent Capri home and he decided to stay back with me in case that green truck decided to show again. I couldn't wait to get home and wrap my arms around Sunshine. These few hours of not seeing her really made me miss her crazy ass. I was slowly falling in love with a chick I met almost a month ago.

Stash pulled into my driveway.

"Yo my nigga, check that out."

"What?" I turned and looked in the direction of him pointing.

"Oh shit!" I jumped out the car and ran to the door. There was glass everywhere.

"Camilla!! Camilla!! Where you at Sunshine?" I yelled at the top of my lungs.

My heart was now racing; there were drops of blood on the stairs.

I ran up the stairs and searched in every room until I got to my room. It was like a tornado hit the shit, like somebody was looking for something. I noticed the bathroom door wasn't there. I walked in and damn near passed out. I never heard Stash calling me; all I could do was stand there in shock. She was lying there naked, beaten and battered in a pool of her own blood. She had blood from her head and what appeared to be a bullet wound in her chest.

"T, where you at?" Stash yelled as he was walking into the bathroom.

As a solider he was used to seeing shit like this. He immediately jumped into action.

"T, she has a pulse, call 911 now, she's been shot."

Once he said she was alive I took out my phone and called 911.

He took one of the towels and held it down on her chest to stop her from bleeding. I went into the bedroom and snatched the blanket off the bed to cover her body up with it. "I'm not waiting for the ambulance, let's go," I said scooping her up and we ran down the stairs.

Stash was doing 100 down 21 to the hospital. We pulled into the St. Joseph Hospital emergency area ten minutes later. I jumped out with Camilla and ran into the ER.

"Can I get some help?"

Two nurses with a gurney came running my way. I laid her down and ran with them as they rushed her to the back.

They made me wait outside. I felt like turning up on them because I wanted to be with my sunshine.

Stash came walking to the back.

"Did they say anything yet?"

"Nah man, they didn't. Who could have done this man? No one knows where I live. But you ma and my G-ma. I need to find out who's responsible for this man. Did you see her? They fucked her up man. And she was naked, why was she naked? They violated my baby, man," I said pacing back and forth.

"We'll find them man, I promise you, if it's the last thing I do. I'm gonna find them fuckers for you."

"The family of Camilla Baxter."

"That's me doc, how is she?"

"Who are you young man?"

"That's my lady, how is she?"

"She's going to be fine. She was shot in the chest but fortunately the bullet didn't hit and major arteries so we were able to remove it. She has multiple cuts and scrapes, and a dislocated hip. She suffered from a mild head concussion from taking a blow to the head. She could have either been hit with something or slammed really hard into something."

"Doc, can I see her please?"

"Son, listen… I also discovered some disturbing information. Miss Baxter was raped and sodomized. We had to stitch her up. We also administered a few STD tests just in case something was transmitted to her.

Young man, I can tell you cared deeply for Miss. Baxter so I know you didn't do this to her. But we need her next of kin to give us permission to allow you in. Do you have any way of getting in contact with her parents?"

"Uh yea, I can contact her mom."

"Please do that young man. Those officers back there are going to ask you some questions. If you want the person responsible for this to pay, tell them everything you know."

I just looked at him.

"Yea, okay doc." I wasn't telling them shit because I didn't know who could have done this. Even if I did, I wasn't saying anything.

"Sir, I'm Detective Jones. I would like to ask you a few questions. Ms. Baxter was found in your home is that correct?"

"Yes,"

"May I ask your relation to Miss Baxter?"

"Yea, that's my lady."

"Do you know who's responsible for this?"

"No, I don't."

"Do you have any enemies that could have attacked Miss Baxter out of retaliation to get back at you for something?"

"No, I don't." At that moment the green truck came to mind.

"Detective, if you have no more questions, I need to get in contact with her mom."

"Ok, here's my card if you can think of anything."

I took the card and me Stash left. I needed to get to the club to get Camilla's mom number.

The ride to the club was silent. I was too lost in my thoughts to realize that we were at the club already.

"T, she's gonna be okay. From the stories you tell me about baby girl, she's strong and a fighter. She can handle this shit," Stash said, trying to reassure me.

"I know man, I just don't know if she's gonna want to fuck with me anymore. I put her life at risk twice already. We damn near dying on the road. Then this shit. I don't know what I'm gonna do if Camilla leaves man. In this short amount of time she captured my heart, man."

"She ain't going anywhere man, I promise you. And if her ass thinks she's about to get up and leave my boy, she got another thing coming. I'll tie her little feisty ass up some damn where." Stash said causing me to laugh, at the same time giving me a little hope.

We both hopped out the car and walked into the club.

I opened the file cabin that was in my office where I had all of my employees' files. Stash stayed downstairs at the bar talking to Capri.

I found Camilla's file and her emergency contact was listed as Joann Baxter; I assumed that was her mother.

I called the number and a woman answered sleepily.

"Hello Ms. Baxter, my name is Troy Conners. I'm not sure if Camilla told you about me."

"Yes young man, she told me everything about you. I'm assuming since you're calling me seven in the morning, it's not for an introduction. Now what's going on with my baby girl? Where is she?"

"Ms. Baxter, something terrible happened to Camilla. She's in St. Joseph's Hospital. She's doing fine from what the doctor said, but I couldn't see her without your permission."

"Oh Lawd, my baby, I'm on my way up there."

"Ms. Baxter, I'm on my way to get you, just give me your address."

After she ran down her address to me, I grabbed Stash and we headed out the door, hopped in his Audi and were out.

We made it to Paterson in twenty minutes. I made Stash break every driving law on the way there. Ms. Baxter was outside pacing back and forth. I could tell she was crying because I could see the dry tears on her face. I hopped out and walked towards her.

"Troy?"

"Yes ma'am?"

"What's going on with my baby?" She asked grabbing onto my face with both hands and staring into my eyes.

"She was attacked. I'm not sure by whom, but I promise I'll find out."

She shook her head and we headed towards the car, as I helped her into the back seat. Ten minutes later, we were pulling up to St. Joe's. I let Ms. Baxter out and gave Stash a dap. Against his wishes, I told him to go home.

"Call me if you need me my hitta, aight?"

"Aight my nigga, catch you lata."

I shut the car door and ran to catch up with Ms. Baxter, who was walking as fast as her legs could go, like she knew where she was going.

We walked in, got our passes and were headed to the back to see her.

"Hi, can you tell the doctor of Camilla Baxter that her mom is here."

"Sure, no problem." The nurse said.

Minutes later, the doctor came walking out to us and we shook hands again.

"Hello Ms. Baxter, I'm Doc—" he was cut off.

"Look, just tell me where my damn baby is."

"Yes ma'am. I must warn you she's been beaten pretty badly."

We walked into the room and Ms. Baxter damn near fainted when she saw Camilla. I caught her before she hit the ground.

"Lawd, Jesus, who did this to my baby Troy?" she cried and I just hugged her. I walked her over to the chair and sat her down. I walked over to Camilla and I felt like crying; I felt like this was all my fault. I should have never sent her home without me. I knew someone was out to get me, how could I do something so stupid? I grabbed her hand and kissed it. I pulled up a chair and sat there next to her. I needed for her to wake up.

Ms. Baxter and I sat there for hours. She was reading her bible and I just sat there planning my next move, finding out who did this shit.

My phone vibrated and it was a picture message from an unknown number.

I opened the message and it was a picture of Camilla naked, beaten and bloody.

Who the fuck?

I forwarded the message to Stash. One of his army brothers was good at tracking phones and GPS' and shit. I need to know ASAP who fucked up my baby like this.

I grabbed Camilla's hand and kissed it, and turned back to the TV. I felt Camilla squeeze my hand and when I looked over, her eyes were open.

"Hey baby," she tried to sit up. "Shh, ahh," she winced in pain.

"Don't try and move. You have a broken rib and they had to relocate your hip. So, you're going to be in a lot of pain for a little while, but don't worry, ya man got you, aight Sunshine?"

She gave me a weak smile.

"Look," I said nodding my head towards Ms. Baxter who was sound asleep.

"She's been praying since I picked her up. She's probably exhausted."

"Can you go wake her for me please?" I walked over to Ms. Baxter and lightly tapped her.

She opened her eyes, "Is everything ok, Troy?" she asked.

"Yes ma'am," I said pointing to Camilla.

She jumped up out of her seat and rushed the bed, completely forgetting of Camilla's injuries. I could tell all the pain she was in, but knew her mom needed to hug her.

She finally let Camilla go and sat on the side of the bed.

"I'm so happy you're ok baby," Ms. Baxter said with a tearful voice.

"Don't worry yourself about me Momma, I'm a fighter," Camilla said to her mom.

I interrupted them. "I'm gonna step out for a minute, okay Sunshine? I'll be right back," I said squeezing her hand. She gave me this look like she has to say something but couldn't because her mother was in the room. I kissed her lips and walked out the room.

I stepped out into the hall and pulled my phone out to call Stash.

"Yo, did you get the message I sent you?"

"Yup, Tim is working on it as we speak. How is she doing?"

"She's good man, she just woke up. I'm letting her and her mom get a little time. Hopefully she remembers who the fuck did this shit to her. I'll get up with you though, I'm about to go back in the room."

*****

I hung up the phone and was about to walk into the room when Ms. Baxter came walking out.

"She would like to talk to you about something in private; I'm going to go find the doctor."

"Okay ma'am."

"Didn't I tell you to stop calling me ma'am, it's momma."

She walked off and I walked into the room.

"Hey Sunshine."

"Hey baby."

"How you feeling?"

"Do you really wanna know?" she asked, looking me in the eye.

I lifted her head up. "Yes, I want to know."

"I feel violated, I feel disgusting for what he did to me, and I feel preyed upon. One thing I won't be is someone's victim so I feel like someone has to die when I get up out of here."

She had a look of death in her eyes. I swear I saw the sweet innocent soul of Camilla float out of her body and the person literally staring me in my eyes without blinking was kind of scary and kind of sexy too, but it's too early to try and go there with her.

"I hear you baby and I promise you there will be blood spilled over this. Do you remember who did this?"

Yea, I do… that bitch nigga Supreme. He was the one in the green truck that's been following you and who ran us off the road."

After hearing her say Supreme's name, I was ready to run up out of there hunt him down, but I knew Camilla needed me here for her right now.

Chapter 16

Supreme

After I left Camilla ass lying in her own blood, I had plans to get my ass out of dodge. Keyonna was paying me to kill Camilla which I could have easily done, but I had my own score to settle with Troy. I couldn't collect my money until Camilla was dead and gone. I sat outside of St. Joseph's Hospital waiting for this chick Karla that I was fucking with, who worked inside the hospital. She was supposed to call me when Troy left the room.

I waited for an hour, before I finally saw Troy leave out the hospital and get into a black Escalade. I got out the car and walked into the hospital and straight past the desk. I didn't have to sign in or anything because the night before, Karla swiped me a visitor's pass.

I walked to 410 where Karla said she was located. I looked in the room and the coast was clear. Camilla was sleeping. The plan was to shoot her and be out, but that would cause too much attention. I grabbed a pillow that was sitting on the chair next to the bed and placed it over her face. I held the pillow down with all my strength. Camilla started kicking and fighting to get the pillow off her face. This chick was strong as hell or I was a weak nigga; she was really giving me a fight. I held down even tighter. She was still fighting and scratching. By now I had scratches on my arms and hands. She finally stopped moving and I held down a little longer until I felt something come hard across my head and felt my shit start to leak. I turned around and there was an older woman standing there with a metal bed pan in her hand that she just bust my shit wide open with. I took off running out the hospital out the back exits. Where the hell did this old lady come from? I thought Karla said the room was empty. I'm going to kill that bitch.

I made it to the car and called Keyonna. "Yo, the job is done. I'm coming to get my bread."

"You sure the job is done?"

"Yes I'm sure bitch! Now meet me at Garden State Plaza."

"Hahahahaha, be there in an hour nigga," she said and hung up.

I definitely was out soon as I got my money. I made a quick stop home so that I could pack a few clothes. My gut was telling me to just go meet Keyonna and get gone to Houston, but I ignored it and went home instead.

Ms. Baxter

After I bust the man upside the head with the bed pan and he ran out leaking blood, I hurried to my baby to check her pulse and she didn't have one. I ran out the room yelling as loud as my old lungs could go. I needed them to save my baby girl's life. A few nurses came running into the room. I tried to go in with them but the made me stay outside. I watched from outside the door as they gave her CPR and tried to revive her. I heard clear for the third time and still nothing. My heart sank and I felt myself about to break down, until I heard her heart monitor beep.

"Oh dear God," I let out a sigh of relief.

"What happened?" I heard from behind me and turned to Troy.

I couldn't do anything but break down in his arms.

"We almost lost her Troy."

"What happened? Everything was fine when I left," he said.

"I don't know Troy. I got up to use the bathroom. I washed my hands off and turned off the water and I heard what sounded like grunting. I opened the door Troy, and this man was standing over her with a pillow and she wasn't moving anymore. I picked up the bed pan because that was all I could find and I hit him, Troy," I said breaking down crying.

"It's ok Ms. Baxter; I promise you it'll be ok. Camilla is breathing now and that nigga won't be. Can you describe to me this man you saw?"

"Yes, he was tall and had muscles. He was fair skinned with curly hair."

Troy shook his head, "Ok, I know exactly who that is."

The doctor came out of the room. "She's doing very well. Can you tell me what happened?"

"Yea, some maniac was in here smothering my baby when I came out the bathroom. What kind of hospital is this?"

"Doc, she's right, if she wasn't here, Camilla could have been too far gone for a comeback. I'm taking her up outta here and I'll hire a private nurse to look after her."

"It's against my better judgement but if Ms. Baxter consents to it, I guess I have no right to disagree."

"Thank you, now can you get the discharge papers together doc?"

Chapter 17

Troy

I stepped out into the hallway and pulled out my phone.

"Yo, grab that nigga now!" I yelled over the phone to Stash.

"This fucker just tried to kill Camilla. What the hell is his problem with her? I know this nigga can't be doing all this shit over pussy. When you grab him, take him out to the warehouse I bought out in Newark. He's getting done up tonight!"

I hung up the phone and called to make the arrangements for Camilla to get moved to my house. I wasn't about to risk my baby getting fucked with again.

*****

After getting off the phone I was about to put it into my pocket when it started to vibrate. I looked down at the screen and it was Keyonna.

"What the fuck do you want girl?" I yelled into the phone.

"Oh, I was just calling to check on you, how are things? How's Camilla holding up?" she said.

It sounded kind of suspicious. Why the fuck would she be asking about a bitch that whooped her ass?

"What do you want Keyonna?"

"I wanted to know if we could hook up; I got something I need to tell you."

"Oh yeah, and what is that?"

"About the hit my father has out on you," she replied.

"You talking about a hit, it probably ain't even no fucking hit out, ya thirsty ass just doing this for attention."

"No, I swear. Look Troy, just come meet me. I have information you might want to know, it's up to you. Just hit me up if you wanna link up."

"Yea iight, meet me at the club tomorrow night." With that said I hung up and walked in the room to check on Camilla.

She was up talking with her mother.

"Troy, I wanna leave this place. Like tonight, I mean it."

"Ok Sunshine, anything you want baby girl."

I went out and spoke with the doctor to let him know we were getting up outta here tonight. Once again, he urged Camilla to reconsider staying in the hospital for health reasons and baby girl just wasn't having it. She wanted to be out.

I had Stash come and scoop us from the hospital. I was wheeling Camilla out in the wheelchair and one of the nurses at the nurse's station was giving me a shitty look. I ignored it and left out the door. Stash was waiting outside for us.

"Hey sis, you good?"

"Yea I'm good, just ready to go home."

"Aight, let's go."

I lifted Camilla out the wheelchair and into the car. I pushed the chair to the door and hopped in.

After getting Camilla squared away in the guestroom and making sure Ms. Baxter was good, I took out my cell phone and call Keyonna. I wanted to know what the hell she was up to. We agreed to meet at the club.

I pulled into the parking lot and it was empty. After everything that happened, from the fire to the garage, to Camilla being attacked, I decided to close the club down for a week. I wasn't focused enough at this point to run a business. I gave everyone paid time off. I unlocked the doors walked in and looked around to make sure there was no one around. I locked the door back and headed upstairs to wait on this chick. I opened my office door, cut the lights on and walked in. I felt something sharp go into my neck. I turned around and it was Keyonna standing there with a syringe in her hand. I grabbed this bitch by her neck lifted her off her feet and slammed her into the wall.

"How the fuck did you get in here?"

"I still have a key; you thought you were just gonna get rid of me that fast?"

I tightened my hands around her neck and I felt another syringe go into my neck.

I started to become weak. I dropped Keyonna to the floor and started walking backwards to the couch because I felt my legs about to give out. And they did just that as I made it to the couch. She started walking towards me. I lost all control of my body. She started undressing herself and walked to her pocketbook and took another syringe out. What was this bitch trying to do? I already couldn't move, what more did she want? She took the syringe and stuck it into my dick, causing my shit to get hard as a brick. What the fuck did this chick have planned?

She sat down on my dick and started riding me. I was pissed when I realized she was fucking me without a condom. I was really being raped. This was nuts.

She got off of me and started sucking my dick. She jumped back on and started riding me in a reverse cowboy position. I wish I could have gathered the strength to choke this bitch. If Camilla was to find out she would kill Keyonna's ass. After riding me and forcefully sticking her tongue down my throat, she started moaning as if she was cumming. This bitch was really getting off from this shit. She started to slow her pace. She got up off me and she stood in front of me. I couldn't do anything but lay there. She wiped herself and put her clothes back on. She kissed me, grabbed her pocketbook and walked out leaving me there with my dick hanging out.

I sat there for a few minutes before I started getting some kind of feeling in my legs and hands. I sat up and tried to stand myself up, but I lost my footing and fell back on the couch. I pulled out my cell phone and called Stash.

"Yo, I need you to come to the club."

An hour later Stash came walking into the club. I finally managed to get up and was sitting at my desk drinking water.

Whatever it was that Keyonna put in my system had me feeling dehydrated as hell.

"Yo what's good?"

"You won't believe what this bitch Keyonna did."

After telling him the whole story, he got up, went down to the bar and brought up a bottle of Hennessey. "Here nigga cause you need this. I can't believe that bitch raped you, nigga," he started laughing, but I didn't find that shit funny. I was ready to kill this bitch. But she was going to have to wait until I handled this nigga Supreme. I think I might save her for Camilla. Let her hand over another ass whooping to this bitch.

2 months later

Camilla

It has been two months since I had discharged myself out of the hospital. I had been staying at Troy's house recovering with the help of my mom and the nurse Troy had hired. I was 80% better, I just had pain when I tried to move too fast from the broken rib I had. Other than that, I was perfectly fine. The nurse and my mom wasn't needed anymore; they were just becoming a pain in my ass. Not to mention Troy smothering me. I understand he felt like what happened to me was his fault, no matter how many times I tried to convince him it wasn't. I was staying in one of the guestrooms because Troy's bed was too high. Troy had literally filled the whole room with roses. Every day he went out and came back in with another dozen of roses. It was starting to become too much. Literally, my allergies couldn't handle it anymore.

I needed to get out this house. I called Capri to see what she was up to and for her to come pick my ass up. Capri and I had become super close. I didn't have friends so she was kind of my one and only. Kitty had been ignoring my calls for these last two months.

Capri would see her at work and tell her I was trying to get in touch with her and she would just say ok and still ignore my calls. I don't know what I did to her, but I honestly didn't care. Bitch couldn't even call and check up on me after what I had been through.

"Yo bitch, what you doing?"

"Shit girl, just putting the last load of laundry in. What ya cripple ass up to?"

"Bitch, call me cripple again, I'ma kick yo' ass. I ain't doing nothing, bored out my mind and Troy isn't here."

"Aww, you missing ya man?"

"Actually, no I'm not; I need a break away from his crazy butt. If he not blocking my sinuses with these damn flowers, he's stuffing my face with food and making me drink so much water I feel like my organs are floating around in my body. Come kidnap me, please before he comes back, pleeeaassse?" I begged.

"Girl, every night Stash has been coming home with blood on his clothes. I wanna know what his ass up to that I have to keep washing blood out of his clothes. I ask but he doesn't say shit."

"Yea, Troy too. What the fuck them two psychos up to?"

"Priii," I whined, "come get me."

"Girl shut up, I'll be there in an hour."

"Okay."

After hanging up with Capri, what she said about Stash coming home with blood on his clothes really had me curious. I wanted to know what their asses were up to.

I slowly climbed out of bed and went to Troy's room; well, our room so he says, to get something to wear. I barely had anything there. The night I was attacked, Troy was supposed to take me shopping that following morning. I grabbed my Bebe tights with the matching Bebe crop top, some underwear out the Victoria's Secret bag and went to take a shower.

Getting undressed was painful as hell. I almost wished that I hadn't sent my mom and the nurse home. I tried taking off the t-shirt but because of my healing ribs, I couldn't do it. I went to the drawers and grabbed the scissors and just cut the damn shirt off. Mission accomplished. I had hooked my iPod to my Beats Pill and had my Tinashe album playing.

Troy had gotten the vanity mirror fixed, so I stood there and was just staring at myself. All of the bruises on my body and face had cleared. I was semi back to my old self. I haven't been able to work out and lying in that bed all day caused me to gain weight. It wasn't bad weight because it has all gone to the right places. My hips had spread and thighs had thickened. I was now perfectly proportioned. Before, I had little ass toothpick legs carrying a gigantic ass, looking like Kim Kardashian.

"Hey sexy."

I looked up and into Troy's beautiful eyes.

"Hey baby, how long have you been standing there?"

"Long enough."

"You're such a creep."

I was just admiring your beauty. You're sexy as hell, ma," he said making me blush. He started walking toward me. He wrapped his arms around my waist and kissed me on my neck and my coochie started to become wet immediately. He knew that was my spot. I threw my head back in ecstasy. He started pinching and squeezing my nipples and I couldn't control myself. I turned around and kissed him passionately. I missed this nigga and more than anything, I missed that dope ass dick he had. My hands found their way into his basketball shorts and into his boxers. King was already hard as a Charms Blow Pop. I grabbed it and pulled it out in one swift move. He grabbed my hand.

"You sure you ready?"

"Yup," I said, and dropped down to my knees and took king in my mouth and down my throat. I didn't realize how much I missed him until this very moment. I missed the feel of him, the smell of him and the taste of him. I could tell he missed me too because not even two minutes into me giving him head, he came down my throat. He picked me up and sat me on the marble countertop. He pulled the bench from the vanity over to sink where I was sitting. He sat down, put both of my legs on his shoulders and started kissing up my thighs nice and slow. He started French kissing the inside of my thighs and that alone had a bitch about to cum. After having this make out session with my legs, his tongue walked down to my clit where he kissed, nibbled and blew on it. He moved down further and started to devour my sweet flower. I don't know what he was doing but whatever it was had my toes curling into the bottom of my feet.

His tongue started to penetrate me and it felt so good. It's been two months without any penetration, and my ass needed to get some kind of penetration. My baby was going in. He grabbed my arms and wrapped them around his neck, all the while my legs were still on his shoulder. I was now sitting on his shoulders with my pussy in his face, and he was still eating without missing a beat. He walked over to the bed and lay down with me sitting on his face. I got myself right and started to ride his face like I was riding his dick. His nose was rubbing my clit. I felt like I was about to explode. I felt the biggest orgasm of my life coming. I started winding my hips against his face faster and I couldn't control myself; I came all over his face. I was exhausted but I managed to climb down and on top of his dick. I gave him the ride of his life. I missed having this dick up inside of me and I can tell my baby missed my ass too. We freaked each other for about an hour in every position I was able to accomplish. I couldn't do much because of my ribs but I still got it done.

Once we were done we both lay there out of breath.

"You know I love you right?"

"I love you too, baby," I said reaching over and kissing him.

We both got up to go take showers. We washed each other and somehow managed to get another sex session in.

After taking a shower, I lotioned my body put on my clothes and sprayed myself with my American Eagle Vintage perfume. I brushed my hair down and put on some lip gloss. Troy was already dressed and disappeared on my ass, but I knew exactly where he was at.

I walked up the spiral staircase that led up to his office, and tapped on the door lightly before walking in.

"Hey Sunshine, what's up?"

"I'm about to go out with Capri."

"No the hell you not with that tight ass outfit on!"

"What you mean, you brought this tight ass outfit?"

"Yea, two months ago Sunshine. Baby, you know you put on a few pounds, which is not a bad thing 'cause I think it looks sexy. But that shit tight as hell.

"I have nothing else to wear."

"I'll take you shopping tomorrow Sunshine."

I sat there with my arms crossed and lips pouted. Troy got up and walked over to me and wrapped those strong arms around me.

"Fix your face I promise baby, shopping spree on me ma."

"Ok." I turned to walk out the office and he smacked me on my ass.

I stopped in my tracks and did a little twerk for him.

"Dammnn, look at that ass," he said and I walked out the office.

I made it downstairs just in time to hear the doorbell ring. I looked at the screen to see that it was Capri before opening the door.

"Hey bitch!"

"Hey trick!"

"We out or what?"

"No, dickhead up there talking about my outfit too small."

"Well bitch, your outfit is kind of tight. Ya ass is about to spill out and the shit giving you a mean ass camel toe."

"Same thing I said," I heard Troy say from behind me.

"You still down here complaining?" he said walking up behind me and pressing me into the countertop.

"Ooouucchh, you jerk, that hurts!"

"Get off her nigga, 'fore you get jumped in this bitch," Capri said.

"Shut up big face," Troy said playfully mushing Capri in the face. "Where ya man at anyway?"

"Somewhere waiting on yo' ass. Let me find out y'all been linking up with some bitches, I'm gonna shoot the shit outta Stash then hand Cami the gun and let her shoot yo' ass!"

"You ain't gotta hand me shit, I stay strapped," I said pulling my chrome desert eagle from under the countertop.

"Y'all shut up with that shit, we handling business. I'll catch y'all later," he said taking one of my cherries out my bowl and walking out the door.

As Troy was leaving out the door, Pri gave me a look and I automatically knew what she was thinking.

"I'm down if you down."

We both got up and ran to the door.

I looked out and Troy was on the phone. I walked out acting like I was checking the mail. I waved at him and shut the door.

I noticed that there was a DVD in the mail but I didn't have time to check it out. I threw it on the table and looked out to see Troy pulling off. I grabbed my shoes and both of us was out the door. We jumped in the car and Pri put the pedal to the metal and we were out.

We stayed a few cars behind so that we wouldn't be seen.

He jumped on Route 21 on his way to Newark. We were driving for about fifteen minutes before Troy pulled up into the parking lot of a warehouse.

We waited until he got out the car before we pulled into the parking lot and Capri got out.

"Let's go bitch."

"Wait, I gotta put my shoes on."

"Why you just now putting ya shoes on, we were the car for twenty minutes?"

Bitch, nobody told you to have these plush ass carpets. Shit felt good on my feet."

I finally got my shoes on and we walked quietly into the building. We checked every room on the first floor, but they were all empty.

We walked up the stairs on the second floor and we looked in every room expect one. We walked slowly to door.

"Get y'all asses in here," we heard Troy say.

"Ah shit, we caught girl. How the hell did he know?" Capri asked.

"I don't know." I replied

"Did y'all forget I hunt niggas for a living? I noticed your car following me on Route 21. Who else drives a light blue BMW with the license plate TRY ME on it?"

"Shit!" Capri said.

We walked in and I laid eyes on what's been keeping my man occupied.

Chapter 18

Supreme

How the fuck did I end up in this situation man? After I spoke with Keyonna, I should have made my way to the Garden State Plaza to get my money and be my ass on the way to Houston. I just had to make a stop home to get clothes that I could have replaced in Houston. Now I'm sitting here beaten, bloody and naked, missing I don't know how many fingers and toes.

My day had just brightened up when I saw Camilla walk in to the room. She was wearing this tight ass outfit looking sexy as fuck. Even in my predicament my dick still managed to get hard at the sight of her.

Camilla

Walking in and seeing Supreme tied up, I wanted to pull my gun out and shoot him right then and there.

"So this is what you've been up to? Did I not ask you if you tracked down Supreme yet? And you told me no. That's what we doing now Troy? We lying to each other?"

"Look ma, I knew all you had was death to this nigga on your mind. I needed to get some information out of him."

"What information Troy?"

"Someone sent him after me, which caused him to attack you."

I just sat there and stared at him.

I walked up to Supreme. He was tied to a ceiling fan and missing body parts. I got close to him.

"Hello Supreme, didn't think you would be looking into my eyes again, huh? Thought I was dead right? I bet you just want this whole thing to be over with don't you?"

I looked up at him seductively and his dick got hard. "Well, all you have to do is tell us who sent you," I said turning my back to Troy so he couldn't see my next move. I looked down at Supreme's dick and back up to him and slowly gliding my tongue across the top of my lip.

"It was Keyonna who sent me. She wanted me to kill you so that she could take your place."

I turned around and walked back to Troy. "Don't think I didn't see what yo' ass just did!"

"It worked right?" I said walking over to a table that had a machete on it that I assumed was what they used to cut his fingers and toes off. I picked it up and walked back towards him. I stood there for a little while remembering the shit he did to me.

"When I asked you why you were at Troy's house…"

I heard Troy clear his throat.

"Excuse me, our house, you said that you were there to get what you always wanted," I said walking toward him. "Well I'm here today to get what I've been wanting for the last few months."

I grabbed his dick and swung the machete, slicing through his dick like butter. Blood squirted everywhere and I had to jump back so that it wouldn't get on me.

"Oooooooo," I heard coming from Troy and Stash. Capri sat there with a shocked look on her face.

I stood there with this big ass severed dick in my hand, with Supreme screaming like a little bitch. I walked around him and with his own dick, before shoving it up his ass with so much force. Supreme was screaming loudly.

"This bitch is fucking looney," Capri said.

I walked over to the wall and hit the switch to the industrial ceiling fan that Supreme was tied to, and it started to spin.

I took out my gun and took aim. I waited until I had the perfect shot and I fired hitting Supreme right between the eyes. I placed my gun in the back of my waist band of my tights.

"Pri, I'll meet you at the car." With that I walked out the room.

"Un-uh, that crazy bitch ain't getting back in my car."

"I heard that!"

Chapter 19

Troy

The ride home was very quiet. Capri was really serious about not letting Camilla ride with her. I had to admit I was kind of scared too. I knew baby girl had a little crazy in her but damn. After I got the information I needed out of Supreme I was just gonna shoot his ass, but Camilla delivered an even worse punishment. She was right; I should have put her on from the beginning. It would have avoided two months of torture and this awkward silence at the moment.

"Sunshine, I'm sorry. I didn't mean for you to find out that I had caught Supreme. I caught him the same day and I knew you weren't in any shape to be getting revenge on a nigga. Don't think I didn't see how much pain you were in back there. It showed all over your face."

"Troy stop, I get it. I understand you were just looking out for me and I appreciate it baby." She reached over and kissed me on the lips.

"So why you sitting over there so quiet?"

"Just replaying the look on Supreme's face when I cut his dick off… magical moment."

"Uh, yea, you's a psycho chick. I know not to ever hurt you, ma."

We both laughed.

"Shut up nigga."

We pulled up into the driveway. Camilla went to open the car door and I saw her wince in pain.

"Hold up Sunshine, I'm coming."

"Nah, it's okay, grab my new bff, I'm framing that shit," she said talking about the machete she used to cut off Supreme's dick.

We walked into the house, I kicked off my shoes and walked over to the couch and plopped down on it.

Camilla picked up the mail and came and sat down next to me.

"So no more late nights and coming home covered in blood. You know how hard it is to get blood out of clothes?"

"No, I don't. You should have just thrown them out. I could have bought more."

"No, *you* should have thrown them out once you took them off," she said getting up and walking over to the DVD player and putting a disc in.

"What is this we about to watch?"

"I don't know, it came in the mail earlier with my name on it."

She grabbed the remote and pressed play.

I looked up at the screen and the scene in front of me looked all too familiar.

Shit!!! I need to hide that fucking machete quick.

Camilla

Looking up at the screen, all I could see was two dead corpses fucking.

"So when did this happen?" I asked calmly.

"The same day I caught Supreme."

"Two months ago, huh? When I was lying up in this bitch recovering you was out fucking this bitch?

"Camilla, the bitch drugged me. She stabbed me in my neck with some shit that had me unable to move. As you can see I haven't moved not once. Since we've been fucking Camilla, when have you known me to just sit there?"

He was right; I was so blinded by visions of me blowing both of their brains out that I didn't even notice Troy wasn't moving at all.

"So, first this bitch tries to get me killed and now this hoe raped my man. I got something for that bitch. Bae, let me get to the keys to your car."

"Where the hell you going?"

"I have to go to the club and look at some of the dancers' files. Oh, and just so you know, this is about cost you."

"What you mean it's about to cost me?"

"You'll see, now give me the keys."

"Follow me," he said.

We walked out to the garage.

"This has been sitting here for some time, waiting on you."

He walked over to the covered car that I noticed the night Supreme attacked me. He removed the tarp and uncovered a 2015 Audi R8 Spyder, all black with Giovanni rims with CJ engraved on them.

"What does CJ stand for?"

"This," he said and I turned around to Troy down on one knee with a 5-ct. Monique Lhullier princess cut, three-stone Halo diamond ring in his hand.

"Camilla, baby girl, I love the hell out of you. I love everything about you from your peasy ass kitchen to the corn on your baby toe."

"Shut up stupid head," I said with tears in my eyes and smacking him on the top of his head.

"Will you do me the honors of becoming Camilla Edith Jones?"

"Yes!" I jumped up and down.

He placed that big ass flawless rock on my finger and I jumped on him and we both fell to the floor of the garage.

"If I didn't have business to handle I would do you so good on this floor."

"What business you got to handle?"

"I gotta handle the bitch that raped my man," I said while straddling Troy.

"Why don't you save that shit for later and come show your fiancée what that mouth like."

"Boy shut up, I'm still mad at you for not telling me what that bitch did in the first place. Now give me my keys so I can take her out for a spin."

"What, these?" he asked holding the keys up. I went to reach for them but he put them inside his boxers.

"You want them you got to go get them."

I reached down in his pants, squeezed his dick and grabbed the keys.

"Ahh, what you do that for woman? I should shoot yo' ass!"

"And you gon get shot back nigga."

I got up and hit the alarm to unlock the doors and hopped in. I just sat there for a little bit just admiring this fly ass car and this big beautiful ass ring. I couldn't believe I was gonna be Mrs. Troy Jones.

I finally pulled off, heading towards the club.

Funny thing, I called myself testing the speed on my new whip and dumb me got pulled the hell over.

Oh well, I made it to from Montclair to Elizabeth in fifteen minutes; normally it would take about twenty-five to thirty minutes.

I walked into the club and went straight to Troy's office. I had this whole plan in my head and I was ready to put it in action.

I pulled out a couple files for the dancers and wrote all their numbers down.

After making some phone calls, I got five of the dancers down for my plan once they heard how much of an advancement Troy was about to hit them off with.

I put all the files back and made my way down the elevator. When I got off the elevator, something didn't fell right. It seemed darker than when I came up the stairs. I became nervous and tried to power walk to the exit. I heard a noise and was about to take off until the lights came on and people screamed "Congratulations!" I looked around and saw everyone that I knew from my mom, to G-Ma and even some of the bar staff.

I covered my mouth and tried to stop the tears from coming from my eyes.

"How did you guys know I would be here to set all this up?"

"We didn't baby, it was supposed to be at G-Ma's house but when Troy said you were on your way here, everyone made a detour and came here. You got here faster than I anticipated," Capri said.

"Yea girl, did you see my fly new whip my baby brought me?" I said walking over to Troy and hugging him then giving him a kiss on the lips.

"I love you, baby."

"I love you too, Sunshine."

We partied and celebrated until about four in the morning.

Troy and I both hopped in our cars and he followed me home.

We made love for hours until we were both too sore to move a muscle. We couldn't even find the strength to get up and shower at that moment.

Chapter 20

Troy

"Baby hurry up, I don't see what's taking you so long to get ready. You only have like four outfits to choose out of."

"Shut up, I'm ready and you right, I only have four outfits that's why I'm about to light that black card on fire. Let's go."

We got in my car and we were out.

"I have to make a quick stop before we go shopping, aight?"

"All right."

"Yo Don, I'm outside."

Donny was the person I bought all my cars from. He knew my taste and knew I only preferred black cars.

The gate came up and I drove into the underground garage. Camilla and I got out and got on the elevator to the top floor. The elevator opened up and Don stood there waiting on us.

"TJ my boy, what's good with you?" he said in his Sicilian accent.

"Not much Donny; look, I have someone I want you to meet. This here is my baby, my fiancée Camilla.

"Fiancée? When did this happen? Bellisimo" he said in Italian and kissed her hand.

"Aight, enough of that dude," I said grabbing Camilla's hand.

"What's up with you?"

"Come let me show you what's up," he said walking towards a car he had covered in a satin cover. He pulled it off.

"A 2016 Range Rover sport, custom built 85,324, picked especially for you my boy."

"Ok, ok, nice," I said walking around the truck and looking inside of it. "What else you have for me?"

"Alright now, prepare yourself 'cause this baby is beyond magnificent."

He pulled the cover off and I felt like I was hit in the chest with a 2x4.

"A 2016 Acura NSX; as of now, only two exist."

"Daammnnn baby, this car goes hard. I can't wait to drive this," Camilla said.

"Uh no, you won't be killing yourself in my shit. Don't think I don't know about the speeding ticket you got yesterday."

"How you know stalker?"

"I know people in the department," I said not taking my eyes off the beauty in front of me.

"Donny what them numbers looking like for this baby?"

"It's 155,136 dollars."

"Nice, I'll take them both. You know where to have them delivered. I'll have the money transferred over to you. It should be more than enough for both the cars and your finder's fee."

"You always look out for the old man."

"Of course. Aight, we out Donny."

After leaving Donny's, we made our way to my mom's shop. She had only the best top designer clothing and that's what my baby was going to get. She was cheap so I know she was thinking we were going to the mall.

Pulling up to the shop, the first thing I noticed was Kayla's green '98 Honda Accord. I already knew it was going to be a problem.

"Sunshine, do me a favor baby and leave your gun in the car."

"No, why?"

"I just feel like it's best that you leave your gun in the car baby."

"No," she said looking me dead in the eyes as she got out the car.

"Shit!!" Lord please don't let my baby commit any murders inside this shop, please. I got out and we walked into the store.

My mom was the first to greet us.

"Hey y'all," she said running up to Camilla first and kissing her then reaching over and kissing me on the cheek.

"Come on in, Troy told me y'all were coming today, and I had a few thing picked out especially for you," my mother said walking Camilla into the salon section of the shop.

"Hey everybody, I want y'all to meet someone. This is Camilla, my soon to be daughter-in-law. Her and Troy are getting married," she said holding Camilla's left hand up so everyone could see the ring.

There was clapping and "awws" and "congratulations" all around the room except in one area. This bitch—

"Ha, yea, ok!" we heard come from Kayla's hating ass.

"Don't start, Kayla," my mother said.

My mother really hated her so I don't know why she still had a job.

She got up out her chair with her stank ass walk and came up to me. I shook my head and pushed her back. I think you need to back up Kayla.

"What?" she asked.

"You heard him," Camilla said, now standing there with her hands on her hips.

"That's right girl," TaTa the queen of the salon said cheering Camilla on.

"Mind ya business, TaTa," Kayla said. "And who the fuck is you?"

This chick really doesn't know what she got herself into by coming over here.

"I'm his fucking fiancée hoe. I know ya skank ass ain't miss this big ass rock."

"Whatever, he'll be single again. Ya young ass don't look like you know how to keep him."

Camilla looked at me and I begged her to just ignore Kayla and thank God she did and walked back over to my mother.

"Come on Ma, before I catch a case up in here," Camilla said walking away with my mom.

"And you," she said to me, "don't get shot."

"Go on with that shit," I said.

Camilla

"Ma, these clothes are amazing. You picked these out for me?"

"Yes I did. My son only wants the best for you baby girl. I can't have you walking around in clothes from Mandees."

"Hold up, what's wrong with Mandees?"

"Nothing, but if you going to be on my son's arm you have to look the part or you'll be looking just like that hoe, Kayla."

I shook my head. She was right. I was about to be someone's wife; I couldn't continue to walk around looking cheap.

I tried on this amazing black Dior bandage dress. I turned around in the mirror and got dizzy for a minute.

"Whoa!"

"You ok baby girl?"

"Yea ma, I'm ok, I just got dizzy."

"Sure you not pregnant?"

"Yes I'm sure woman. I know how you and G-ma beasting for some grands and great grands; not gonna happen, at least not now anyway."

"Uh huh, ok," she said.

After spending about an hour trying on clothes and shoes, and Ma packing me at least eight bags of clothes, I was ready to go to Victoria's Secret and get me some new sexy underwear for my baby.

I went back to the salon and he wasn't in there.

Where the hell did this boy go?

I walked to the back and I heard voices coming from out a room. The door was open so I walked in. I had seen the bitch Kayla trying to put her hands down Troy's pants. I wasn't having that shit. I yanked the bitch by her hair and swung her to the ground. I hopped on top of her and started throwing blows to her head face, ribs, anywhere I can get an opening. I even punched that bitch in her titty. I felt myself being lifted into the air and she found her opportunity to get away. Instead of her running out the door of the shop, she runs into the salon and tries to hide in the bathroom. I got loose from Troy and walked to the bathroom door and started banging on the shit.

"Bring yo' ass out here. I warned you to stay away from him and ya dumb ass ain't listen."

I banged a few more times until I hurt my hand, and I became even more pissed. I pulled out my gun and shot the door knob off. Thank God she wasn't standing there because she would have been a shot up hoe.

I dragged her out the bathroom, and in the middle of the salon with my gun in my hand, said, "Now for all you bitches that's hard of hearing…"

"Oh un-uh, who she calling a bitch?" I heard TaTa say.

"This nigga here," I said pointing to Troy, "is off limits. Try me and end up like this bitch. Come on baby," I said smacking him on the ass. I knew he hated when I did that shit.

"Don't be smacking me on the ass like I'm some bitch," he said.

"Ma, I apologize for disrespecting business."

"Don't worry about it; your man will get everything your crazy done messed up fixed. "That girl there needed her ass beat a long time ago." Ms. Monica said.

Troy paid his mother, grabbed my bags and we left out.

Chapter 21

Troy

"Did you have to beat that girl up like that?"

"Did she have to grab yo' dick?"

"That's what hoes do," I said.

"Well, she needs to find another nigga dick to grab or next time I'm chopping the bitch's hands off. Let her try me again, Troy. I'm gonna have her tied up next to Keyonna."

"Ha ,"he laughed, "you's a wild girl baby. Where you wanna go next?"

"I wanna stop and check on my mom first then we can go to Garden State Plaza."

"Ok baby, anything for you."

"I love you baby," she said before she laid her head back in the chair and enjoyed the ride to Paterson.

We pulled up to the house in fifteen minutes. Camilla used her key to get in.

"Hey momma," she walked up to her mom who was sitting in a recliner and kissed her.

"Monica, they just walked in, I'll call you back."

"Hey momma," I said reaching over to kiss her cheek.

"What you and my mother on the phone gossiping about?"

"Oh nothing, old woman stuff. Cami baby, come here," she said reaching with both hands and pulling her up and spreading Camilla's arms. She walked around Camilla.

"Momma what are you looking for?"

"Oh nothing," she said with a smile on her face. "You can sit baby, you hungry?"

"No momma," Camilla said.

"Troy?"

"No momma, I'm good.

"Ok, what brings y'all here? Y'all got something to tell me?"

"Something like what?"

"Oh ok, just checking. Cami, why you out here beating people down? I just got off the phone with Monica and she said you whooped on some thot, what the hell is a thot anyway?" she asked.

"She touched my man, Momma, after I already warned her to stay away," Camilla said with her eyes close, like she was ready to fall asleep.

"Well it's not safe for you to be fighting?"

"Why isn't it Momma?"

"You know why, don't think Monica ain't tell me about you getting dizzy at the shop today."

"Oh boy. I'm changing your number; you and Monica don't need to be having each other's numbers."

I was lost as to what they were talking about. I had zoned out a little but I was still able to hear what they were saying.

I was reading a text message in my phone I received from Stan talking about he hadn't heard from Keyonna since yesterday, and how he's been calling her phone and it's going to voicemail. He started making threats but I wasn't fazed by them.

Then the conversation I had with Camilla earlier dawned on me. I was going to wait until we left to question her.

After sitting there for an hour, we gathered our things and said our goodbyes, and got in the car.

"Sunshine, is there anything you want to tell me?"

"Oh boy not you too," she said. "I'm not pregnant Troy, our mommas are bugging."

"What? I wasn't talking about that. I mean this…" I pressed play on the voicemail and played her the message. "What was that you said earlier about having Kayla tied up next to Keyonna?"

"Oohhhhh yea," she had the nerve to say.

Camilla

God dammit, I got caught. I couldn't lie because Troy somehow always knew when I was lying. He was eventually going to find out.

"Yea, I have her and he won't be seeing her boney ass no more. Once the guys are done with her, I'm blowing the bitch's brains out FYI, so I would suggest you handle that nigga because once he realizes she ain't coming back no more, he may come after you baby."

"I ain't worried about that fool. My concern is why the hell you ain't tell me? And when in the hell did you have time to catch her ass?" he asked.

"I didn't, I hired someone to do the dirty work for me."

"When was this?"

"Yesterday, now can we please go to the mall? I have a taste for some California Rolls and I want some new body spray from Bath and Body Works."

"Yea aight, this ain't over," he said.

He already knew I was trying to avoid any more talk about that boney bitch.

My plan was to let the guys have fun with her for a few days then off her ass. I might torture her just so I can hear her beg for her life. I don't know, I guess it depends on how I feel.

We got to the mall and I ran all through the stores from Vicky's to American Eagle. Troy didn't see why I needed to go into clothing stores but I needed jeans and sweat suits. I didn't feel like being all dressed up every day. By the time we were done, I spent over two-thousand dollars, which didn't dent Troy pockets not even a little bit.

We stopped and got my California Rolls and left the mall.

"Alright, now tell me where we going."

"Home, I guess."

"No we're not."

"So if you know where we're going, why ask me?" I said stuffing my face with a roll.

"Where's Keyonna?"

"In her skin."

"Camilla, stop fucking playing with me girl."

"Fine! Get on 21."

After running down the directions to Troy, he must have realized where he was going.

"Really?" he asked.

"What?"

"You have her here?" he asked, referring to the same warehouse he held Supreme for two months without telling me.

"Yup, she's in there."

"And whose car is that?"

"Probably one of the guys I hired," I shrugged.

"What? Camilla, get out the damn car."

"Ugh," I said then finally got out the car.

We went up to the second floor and into the same room.

I was really impressed the guys I hired, who were also dancers at the club, actually pulled it off.

We walked into the room and there was a mattress on the floor and Keyonna was lying there drugged, tied up and naked.

Onyx was putting on his shirt when we walked in.

"Hey Onyx, did you have fun?" I asked tapping him on the shoulder.

"You know I did. Hey boss man, thanks for that bonus, I could really use it," Onyx said before walking out.

"What bonus is he talking about?"

"Oh, you gave a few of the guys a little extra in their checks to help me out with my little plan."

"What plan Camilla?"

"You're looking at it. I hired them to drug this bitch and have sex with her against her will, like she did you," I said giving him two love taps on the cheek.

"Then what Camilla?"

"Oh, I'm going to let this go on for a few more days then kill her ass. Might suffocate her like Supreme did to me, maybe drown her. Let her feel her last breath before it leaves her body."

"So what, you gonna do it or have one of your little minions do it?"

"I don't know yet."

"You're sick."

"I know. Let's go I'm sleepy."

Chapter 22

Kitty

I had been following Troy and Camilla for the last two hours. I knew they had something to do with Supreme's disappearance. What Camilla and Capri didn't know was that I'd been fucking Supreme for a few months. I fell in love with him. To see him so thirsty over Camilla's ass, had a bitch in jealously mode. I started to slowly dislike Camilla day by day. When I heard what happened to her, I felt like she deserved it, that's why I didn't call and check on her. I heard around the bar that Supreme did it and then he went missing. I knew they had something to do with it. I followed them to this warehouse in Newark. I parked around the corner and snuck into the warehouse. I started to make my way up the stairs until I heard someone coming downstairs. I hid on the side of the stairs and noticed that it was Onyx coming down.

What the fuck is he doing here?

Once he was out the door, I walked up the stairs and peeked around the corner of this big room.

I saw Camilla and Troy standing next to a mattress and someone was lying on it naked.

Camilla and Troy turned to leave and I hid in the shadows outside of the door. I waited until I heard the car door shut and them pull off.

I walked into the room and up to the bed, and noticed who it was they had tied up.

Camilla

2 weeks later

"Yo, yo, yo where the food at?" Troy asked walking into the house.

"Yea, where the food at?" I followed up.

"Don't be coming up in here with all that damn hollering, I told yo' black ass about that shit before," G-ma said .

This woman was a trip; she stayed cursing people out.

"G-ma, why you so mean?" I asked her.

"Who mean? I'm not mean. I'm an angel," she said with a big fake ass smile.

"The devil is a lie," I said to her. "You need help with anything, I'm starving."

"I bet you are; you eating for two, of course you gonna be starving."

"I'm not eating for two, I'm not pregnant. I took a test and it was negative, thank you very much."

"Yea ok, don't trust them fake ass dollar store tests."

"Whatever," I said taking a piece of bacon and walking into the living room with Troy.

"Baby, tell your grandmother to stop harassing me."

"G-ma, leave my baby alone!"

"Shut the hell up nigga, don't tell me what to do in my house!"

"Hey y'all," we heard Capri come in with Stash following close behind.

Fifteen minutes later, Ma came walking in followed by Ms. Viv, who was Capri's grandma and G-ma's sister.

We were all sitting there eating and talking about this big engagement party that Capri wanted to throw for us. I was kind of reluctant at first but then I agreed to it.

"Troy, Aunty is so proud of you baby. You have a successful business and now a beautiful bride-to-be, and I want to thank you for taking care of my grandbaby. Now if only I can get your cousin, Lexington on the straight and narrow, I could die a happy aunt," Viv said.

"When was the last time you heard from my brother grandma?"

"Maybe two months ago. He called me when he got arrested for beating his crackhead girlfriend up. I had to pull some strings and get the charges thrown out. Next time I think I might let him go to jail, just so I know he'll be safe."

"I'll check up on him aunty, where he staying?"

"Out in Brooklyn."

"Ok, cool."

As they were talking, my phone started to vibrate and I looked down and to my surprise, it was Kitty calling. I got up and went out on the porch.

"What's up stranger?" I said answering the phone and putting it on speaker.

"Hey Camilla, how are you?"

"Oh, now you concerned about me? Bitch bye!" and I hung up. I started to walk back in the house but the phone rang again.

"What do you want Kitty?"

"I'm just calling to apologize; I haven't been a good friend to you. I should have called to check on you, I just couldn't believe that happened to you and I feel like if I had seen you or spoke to you it would have confirmed the truth. I'm so sorry Camilla; if I ever see Supreme I promise I'm killing his ass.

"Oh that nigga won't be a problem where he's at."

Kitty got quiet. "Hello?"

"Yea, I'm here, sorry girl."

"Alright listen, I accept your apology but look, I'm having breakfast with Troy's family. I'll give you call later about the details for this engagement party Capri supposed to be throwing for us and FYI bitch, you're going to be my bridesmaid; talk to you later boo."

I walked in the house and everyone was still sitting at the table talking about the engagement party.

"Everything alright baby?"

"Yup, everything is cool, that was Kitty."

"What that hoe want?" Capri asked.

"She wanted to apologize for not calling and checking up on me. I asked her to be a bridesmaid."

"What? Bitch, you ain't ask me, I'm your maid of honor and the wedding planner.

"And I'm the bride Capri, damn. She said she was sorry."

"Well I don't trust the bitch, but ok."

"Cool,"

"So did you guys pick a wedding date?"

"Yup, December 31st."

"That's only three months away! Camilla, how you expect me to plan a wedding in three months?"

"Well, I can always hire a wedding planner."

"Don't insult me bitch, I got this. Prepare to be amazed."

"Ok, don't be trying to throw me no ghetto ass sunflower seeds, pickles and grape drink wedding."

We sat there for a few more hours talking about the engagement party and the wedding. Troy didn't want to be a part of it, he just wanted the bill. I wasn't used to having thousands of dollars at my fingertips, so if it was up to me I would have thrown myself a wedding for less than 20,000 dollars, but Capri wasn't sparing any expense. Once she was through with this wedding planning, I think me and Troy were going to have to get jobs as strippers.

"Alright, we're about to get out of here," Capri said, "but be ready tomorrow, we're going dress shopping."

"Oh, don't worry about that, I had a collection of Vera Wang dresses sent to the shop; it should be arriving in the morning."

"See Aunty, that's why you're the bomb, you be on it girl," Capri said kissing Ms. Monica on the cheek.

"How did you manage to get a collection of Vera Wang dresses woman?" I asked.

"Money talks."

"Oh, so I don't get no credit?" Troy asked from the living room, never taking his eyes off the TV screen.

"It was Troy's idea to have them sent and I put in the calls."

"Don't be taking my baby's credit," I hit Ms. Monica softly on the arm. I walked into the living room and Troy was slouched down in the sofa looking so damn sexy with his fitted hat pulled low and them sexy, plump pink lips. If you didn't know him you would think he was a street thug. I sat on his lap, wrapped my arms around his waist and laid my head on his shoulder.

"I love the hell out of you, you know that?"

"I love you more, Sunshine," he said kissing me on the forehead.

That was the last thing I remember because I drifted off to sleep in my baby's arms.

I woke up to Troy's hand creeping up my shirt. I played sleep until his hand went under my bra and he squeezed my nipple.

"Ouch you perv," I said smacking his hand away.

"What, I though you liked when I played with your nipples?"

"I do, but they're sore right now. Aunty Flow must be on her way."

"Oh yeah?" he asked sarcastically with his arms crossed and his lips twisted.

"Yea, why you looking at me like that?"

"When the last time you had your period, Camilla?"

He actually had me stumped because I really couldn't remember.

"Exactly, stop being in denial and go get checked by a doctor," he said to me.

I hated to admit it but he was right.

I woke up the next morning to my phone ringing off the hook. It was Capri's psycho ass.

"Girl, why are you calling me this early in the morning?"

"Bitch, it is one in the afternoon, what you mean this early in the morning? I've been calling yo' ass since eight so that we could go try them dresses on. Aunt Monica has been calling looking for us."

"Oh shit, I didn't even realize it was this late. I'm getting up now. Give me an hour."

"No, thirty minutes, that's all you getting."

"Alright."

I jumped out the bed and took a ten-minute shower.

I put on my American Eagle distressed boyfriend jeans, a white cropped t-shirt and my metallic blue stilettos. I combed my weave down, slicked some edge control on my edges, grabbed my Ray-Bans and was finished with five minutes to spare to go find my fine ass fiancé.

I walked in his office where I would usually find him, but he wasn't there. However, there were papers and a picture of a kid on the floor; I wondered what happened in here.

I left out and went to search the patio and the rest of the house. Then I remember his cars were supposed to be delivered today.

I walked out to the garage and he was out there playing in his new toys.

"Hey baby," I said walking toward him.

I could tell something was bothering him.

"You looking good ma, where you going?"

"To your mom's shop. Is everything ok?" I asked walking to the driver's side of the Range Rover and standing between his legs.

"Yea, why you asked that?" he responded, pulling me closer by the waist which really hurt.

"I went to the office and there were papers on the floor."

"Oh!"

"Oh? What's up talk to me?"

"We'll talk about that later. But I called your school today and I paid off your tuition."

"You didn't have to do that Troy."

"Well I'm your man, I wanted to do it. You're going to be busy with the wedding and school and…" he looked down to my stomach.

"Boy, shut up, I'm not pregnant," I said hitting him in his head.

"Yea, ok," he replied. "But I don't need you stressing about paying off school. I wanted to lighten your load a little."

"Well, I appreciate you showing concern for me, but I Am Woman, I can handle it." I kissed him and walked away.

"Make sure you make that appointment," I heard him yell before I jumped into Capri's car.

"So what was that the re-re was yelling about?"

"Nothing important."

We pulled off and were on our way to the shop.

"Girl, I forgot to tell yo' ass, I had to beat the shit out of that bitch, Kayla."

"Noooo, bitch when?"

"Two weeks ago."

"What happened?"

"That bitch got disrespectful and I had to straighten that ass up. Troy had to buy Miss Monica a brand new bathroom door and everything. I shot the doorknob right on off and drug that trash right on out."

"You are wild crazy but I love it bitch."

We pulled up to the shop and walked in.

"Hey everybody," we both said.

I looked in the corner at this bitch and she couldn't even make eye contact. I wasn't the only one who noticed. TaTa peeped it and put her blast.

"Oh, don't act like you busy Miss Fish over in the corner. What was all that shit you was popping about you seeing her again, you was gonna what?"

Kayla grabbed her stuff and walked to the back room. Everybody laughed at her punk ass.

"I hope I'm getting an invite to the wedding?" TaTa asked.

"Girl, you doing my hair, so don't make plans for December 31.

"New Year's Eve?"

"Yup!"

"Well I'm charging double, I know Troy got it."

"Aight crazy."

"Ain't *this* the pot calling the kettle black. I'm not the one bodying doors and knocking bitches mute."

This girl was a trip. She had the whole shop in tears.

"I can't deal with you right now, TaTa. Where my momma in law at?"

"In the back hiding something she doesn't want anyone to see."

"Aiight, catch y'all later."

Capri and I walked to the back. As we were making our way to her office, the door swung open and Donny, the Italian car salesman that Troy brought his cars from, was coming out the office.

Capri and I both poked our heads in and Ma was fixing her desk.

"Eww, you nasty." Capri said.

"We know what y'all were doing up in here. I'm telling Troy." I said to her.

"Aight now, listen little girls, mind that business."

Capri and I were both cracking up, because if Troy found out he would have a fit and Ma knew that.

"Let's go to the fitting room," she said fixing her hair.

"Yes, because I'm not going in there," I said with a twisted face.

"Shut it up girl," Ma said pushing me.

We walked into the fitting room.

"Oh my God, Mom, what are you doing here?"

"Girl, she's been here since ten o'clock, waiting on you."

"I'm sorry, I overslept; I didn't mean to keep you waiting."

"It's ok baby, now let's try on some dresses."

"Let's do it!"

I tried on three original Vera Wang dress and didn't like any of them.

I picked the fourth one up with the intentions of not liking it. As I was walking to the dressing room, I felt myself get dizzy again and I stumbled a bit.

What the hell is wrong with me?

"Are you ok baby?" my mother asked.

"Yea momma, I'm good. I'm just a little dizzy, probably from not eating."

I walked into the dressing room and removed the dress I had on and was putting the fourth dress on when my head started to spin. I had to sit down for a minute.

I heard a knock on the door and it was Capri asking if everything was ok.

"Yea, I'm coming out right now."

I walked out the room in the Vera Wang Georgette Mermaid dress and my mom started to crying. Capri covered her mouth and Ms. Monica was standing there smiling.

Based on their reaction, I couldn't wait to see how this dress looked on me.

I turned around and to say this dress was absolutely stunning was an understatement. I felt myself about to cry because I had found my dress. It fit me like a glove.

"This is it," I said and everyone agreed.

After twirling in the dress a few more times, I took it off and handed it to Ms. Monica. I felt myself become dizzy again and I stumbled, hitting the floor and everything went black.

Chapter 23

Camilla

I woke up to a beeping noise and wasn't really sure where I was. When I opened my eyes, Troy was sitting in a chair next to me and I realized I was in a hospital.

"Hey, what happened?"

"You passed out from dehydration, Camilla."

"How did that happen?"

"I don't know, you tell me. Do I need to start babysitting you to make sure your drinking water? You're always on the go Camilla slow your ass down and take time for yourself."

Troy was right; maybe I did need to slow down a bit.

The doctor walked in.

"We have some good news and some bad news. Good news is that your twelve weeks pregnant."

"WHAT?" I said jumping up real quick out the bed. Ouch, shit, I forgot all about my ribs that were giving me pain.

"And that's the bad news. That rib is still not healed and that can cause a potential harm to your baby."

I sat there in shock; I couldn't believe what this doctor had just told me.

Ms. Baxter, I would suggest you take it easy until that rib heals. I prescribed you some prenatal vitamins, it's usually recommended that woman start taking them the first five weeks and seeing as though you didn't know you were pregnant, your baby hasn't been getting the DHA needed to help grow. I would suggest you choose an OB quickly.

Once again, congratulations to the both of you and take care of yourself Miss."

After I sat there stunned and speechless, I finally took a deep breath and looked over at Troy. He had an unreadable expression on his face; was he happy or was he mad? Then his lips started to part and he had the biggest, cheesiest smile on his face.

"You're happy?"

"Yes I'm happy, why wouldn't I be? I knew you were pregnant, you were the only one who ain't know you were."

"What you mean you knew?"

"I knew by the way you felt when I dove up into that thang," he said touching Miss Kitty.

"Well you won't be diving into nothing no more. It's your fault I been getting dizzy and fat nigga."

"Shut up and give your fiancé some love." He wrapped his arms around me and kissed me and if I wasn't already sure, I was sure now this was the man I wanted to spend the rest of my life with.

"I guess I can't get that dress that I tried on today."

"Why not?"

"Because, I'm going to be huge in December."

"Alright, so let's move the wedding up."

"What? Capri will have a damn fit!"

"Forget her! She volunteered to be our wedding planner so either she complies or we hire someone else."

"Ok, so when?"

He pulled out his phone and looked at the calendar.

"How about October 16th?"

"That's cool with me baby."

"Cool. Get dressed, everyone is waiting in the hallway."

"Ah damn, I'm not prepared to tell them I'm pregnant. I don't wanna hear the 'I told you so' and all that other crap.

"Well get ready because we're telling them. They're going to need a reason as to why we're moving the wedding date up."

I finished getting dressed and we walked out into the hallway where everyone was waiting.

"Hey y'all."

"Hey Cami, how you feeling?" Capri asked.

"I'm okay."

Just as I was about to speak, my mom came out with it.

"So how far along are you?"

I looked at her sideways

"How did you know?"

"A mother always knows baby," she said getting up and coming over to me and rubbing my belly.

"That's my grandbaby in there."

"Our grandbaby," Miss Monica got up and came to get me a hug.

"Congratulations you two."

"So now we have a wedding and a baby shower to plan."

Troy finally spoke.

"Speaking of the wedding, we're moving the wedding up so that Camilla can wear the dress that she picked out."

"Hold up, up to when?"

"Next month Pri, so I suggest you get to calling or doing whatever you need to give us an extraordinary wedding."

"How am I going to do that I'm a month Cami?"

"You can do it Pri, so instead of you standing here interrogating me, get to work hoe."

"Fine, you two owe me."

Troy

I lay in bed just staring at her beautiful brown face, and I remembered who she reminded me of. The brown-skinned shorty from the TV show, "The Haves and the Have Nots." But my baby was cuter and had a rocking body. I knew once she had the baby she was going to get thicker.

It had been a few weeks since we found out about Camilla being pregnant. I think I was more excited than she was.

I would always have to remind her to take her prenatal vitamins and drink plenty of water.

Now that she was pregnant, I took on the cooking because her ass was heavy handed when it came to salt, and I wasn't having that. I couldn't risk her giving me, her, and the baby high blood pressure.

I tried to stay in the house as much as possible so that she would stay in with me, but this chick was always on the run.

The minute she wakes up, I'm putting my foot down with her ass. It was time to handle that shit with Keyonna so she wouldn't have any excuse as to why she needed to go out so much.

The engagement party was tonight, so I know she had a lot of shit to do with Capri and now Kitty was coming back around. Those three were thick as Nigerian hair. Something about Kitty disappearing and reappearing didn't sit with me too well. I was going to keep an eye on her. For all I know she could be working with Stan's ass, who has been too quiet. I know some shit was bound to happen soon. That was another reason why I wanted Camilla to stay around me.

"Why is your creepy ass sitting there staring at me in my sleep?"

"Cause you're beautiful."

"You must want some," she said with a sneaky grin.

"If I wanted some I would have taken it while you were sleeping."

"Oh yea? Well I have someone that wants to talk to you face to face."

"Oh yea, and who is that?"

"Come here," she started pushing my head down under the covers. I knew exactly what she wanted and I was more than willing to please my Sunshine. This pregnancy was making Camilla extra horny and I wasn't complaining not one bit.

I moved her panties to the side and started digging her out with my tongue. She tasted so sweet, like Honey Nut Cheerios. I started French kissing her pussy lips and penetrating her opening with my tongue, just how she liked it. I ate her pussy until she tapped out. Even still, I continued to eat her pussy until she started begging me to stop. After I was done she was exhausted, and her lazy ass fell right back to sleep.

I let her sleep for an hour before I woke her up.

"Wake up, don't you have to go meet Capri?"

"Do I have to? I don't feel like it."

"I don't know, what were y 'all supposed to go do anyway?"

"She was taking me to go pick up the dress for the engagement party. Then her, Kitty and me, were going over to the shop to get our massages and get our hair and nails done."

"You don't get any bad vibes from Kitty?"

"No I don't, why?"

"I don't trust her. If she was a real friend to you, Camilla, she would have been there for you, not make up excuses as to why she couldn't come to see you.

How many times has Capri told her you were asking for her and she would just roll her eyes and walk away. If you ask me that that was like a straight fuck you. I could be wrong Sunshine, but just be careful with that girl."

"Ok baby, I'll watch her." With that said, she got up and went to take a shower.

After Camilla left out the house, I called Stash and asked him to come over. I had some things I needed to run past him. I needed advice on how to handle this little situation I got myself into. I really didn't know how I was going to tell Camilla.

I took a shower and got dressed. I went to cook me something light to eat while I waited for Stash.

"My hitta, my hitta."

"My nigga, what's good with you?"

"Shit, what's up with you?"

"Nothing, just chilling, waiting to marry my sunshine."

"I can't believe you're actually getting married."

"Yea man, when you plan on popping the question? You and Capri have been together for how long… two to three years? Y'all should have been married."

"She doesn't want to man. I had a ring and everything picked out for her. She must know I've been trying to pop the question and she always reminds me that she's not ready to get married. I'm just going to do a *Why Did I Get Married?* and slip the ring on her finger and make her ass marry me."

"Hey, sometimes a woman won't know until that ring is on her finger. It's like them engagement rings has magic powers or something. Speaking of superpowers, why the fuck Camilla walked Kayla's ass the other day at Ma's shop. I don't know where my baby got the strength from but she dragged Kayla's skanky ass out the bathroom like Kayla weighed nothing. She fucked Kayla up nigga. I know I definitely have to behave myself because my baby will kill a bitch over my, ass just like I'd pop a nigga for her ass."

"Nigga you lying," he said laughing his ass off. "You have something on your hands."

"For real, she even threatened TaTa's ass like I would really mess with him."

"It's them damn hormones I tell you."

"But yo, check this shit out," I said handing him a bunch of papers. Remember about four years ago, I went out to Atlanta to see that cat Rome about putting in some work? Well, while I was out there I ran into this chick named Linda. I met her while I was coming out the gym, and shorty was alright; you know, nice body, cute face. We hit it off, went out for some drinks and by the end of the night, shorty was damn near molesting my ass. So, I took her back to my room and we got it popping. Before I could even let it be known that I wasn't for a relationship and this was only a one-time thing, shorty beat me to it.

Shit got hot and heavy I didn't realize the damn condom had broken. I tried to hit shorty off with some money to get the morning after pill, and she declined my money saying she could afford to get it herself. Shorty seemed like the level-headed type, like she had things going for herself, so I took her word for it.

I received some papers in the mail the other day and it's a legal letter stating that she recently died from a brain aneurysm and that she has a four-year-old son in which she named me as the father on her death bed."

"Oh shit! So you have a son?"

"Yes man, I have a fucking son, and I don't know how to tell Camilla about this."

"Camilla is a real ass bitch, I don't have to tell you that, that's one of the reasons you're marrying her.

She'll understand that this all happened before her. Don't insult her by thinking she's a narrow-minded, immature chick that can't accept that."

He had a point.

"You right man. Why would I ever think that my baby wouldn't be able to handle it. I'm gonna tell her tonight."

"Did they send a picture of the kid at least?"

"Yea, here."

"Yo, he looks like a fucking mini-clone of you my nigga."

"Word."

"Damn, I'm getting married, have a son that I just found out about, and a baby on the way. I would have never thought this would be my life. You and Capri ever spoke about kids?"

Stash got awkwardly quiet.

"Can I tell you something that can't leave this room?"

"Of course, nigga."

"We tried last year. Capri got pregnant twice last year and miscarried both. The doctor mentioned something about her uterus wasn't strong enough to carry a baby. He mentioned something about her being able to get surgery to help with that, but Capri wasn't having it. She felt like if it was meant to be then it would have happened. I think that's why she didn't want to marry me. I don't know man."

"Don't let that shit stop y'all man. Keep trying, it'll happen."

My phone started ringing. "Speaking of the devil."

I answered my phone putting it on speaker.

"Yooo!"

"Yooo cuzzo, run me them numbers, I gotta pay for Cami's dress for the engagement party."

"Nope," I said and I hung up. She calls every day for my American Express number, her ass should know it by heart now.

She called back.

"Nigga, stop playing with me before I kick yo' ass through the phone."

"Shut up, I'll send you a picture of it so you ain't gotta be calling me every damn day." I hung up with her and sent her the picture.

Camilla

"Pri, this dress is the bomb bitch."

Carpi was really outdoing herself. She picked me out a silver, sequence floor-length Giorgio Armani dress that had a split that came all the way up the thigh. I had to be careful how I moved or Miss Kitty would be exposed, and I didn't need Troy shooting up the whole club because they saw what belonged to him.

"Kitty, how fucking sexy is this dress?"

"This shit is fly as hell girl. Wait until Troy sees you in that shit. He's going to kill Capri for choosing this dress and if you wasn't already pregnant, you would have been after he saw this dress on you."

That caused all of us to crack up laughing because she was right. Pri's ass was dead for making him pay for this dress.

After we paid for the dress, we made our way to TaTa and Red to get our hair done up.

"So what time does the party start? I have to go buy me something cute to wear 'cause I know it's gonna be some fine ass down low men up in there."

"If they down low TaTa, how you gonna know they on the down low?" Red asked.

"Gaydar bitch."

"I guess your *gaydar* had a glitch in the system because you swore up and down that Troy was gay and that he was secretly lusting after your lumps.

I turned around and looked at TaTa.

"Oh girl, that was a long time ago, crazy. Leave that gun where it's at hunty, no need for violence," she said trying to turn me around.

"I knew you wanted my man bitch." She went back to doing my hair.

"And you bitch," she said pointing to Red with the rat tail comb, "yo ass always running that mouth of yours. I'm snatch that tongue right on out. Tryna get a bitch shot up in here. But anyway, what time it start?"

"At seven, why don't you get something from Ms. Monica to wear, Tata?"

"Her clothes too damn expensive and she be acting funny like she don't be wanting to give me a discount. I would slay all the outfits she has in there."

"I'm sure you would boo."

TaTa reminded me of Lavern Cox, the transgender that played in "Orange is the New Black." She's absolutely gorgeous. You would never know she was a man. I'm sure she done tricked a few men and sure she done turned a few of them out too.

"Girl, will you stop moving so much," TaTa said popping me with the comb.

"I can't, my butt hurts, give me a pillow or something. Did you forget I am pregnant?"

"Yea, I kind of did. You're barely showing."

"Yea, but it's hard to sit still, my ass is killing me."

It's been four weeks since I found out I was pregnant. I believe Troy was more excited than I was. Truth be told, I wasn't ready to be anyone's mother. I faked being happy when we first found out.

I wanted to finish school first, get my dream job, and then start a family. I guess it's really nothing that could be done about it now. I noticed the more my stomach grew the more regret I felt. I guess that was why I was in denial when everyone was telling me I was pregnant; it was because I didn't want to be. There was so much going on in my life I wasn't sure how much more I would be able to take.

After we were done getting our heads fried and dyed, I was exhausted and ready to go home and take a nap.

It was now 4:30 and the engagement party was in two and a half hours. I was definitely about to sneak me a nap in.

We stood up to leave but Kitty was nowhere to be found. I went looking for her and found her in the bathroom on the phone. I don't know what the conversation she was having about, but I could hear her tell someone not to fuck up her plan and to be there on time.

"Hey girl, you ready to go?"

She turned around quickly hanging up on whoever she was on the phone with.

"Yup, let's be out," she said.

Something seemed odd about Kitty. Troy's words about her reappearance played in my head. Maybe I do need to keep my eye on this bitch. They say keep your friends close and your enemies closer.

Capri was on her way to drop Kitty off when she asked to be dropped off around the corner from her house. Capri did as she asked.

We said our goodbyes and drove off.

Capri pulled into my driveway and we spoke for a bit. I told her about Kitty's weird behavior and we both agreed to keep an eye on her.

"Alright babe, I'll catch you later."

"Alright girl, have your ass on time please. I got a banging ass grand entrance for y 'all."

"Alright, damn, I'll be on time. Did you forget I'm pregnant?"

"No bitch, that excuse ain't working over here. Be on time Camilla!"

I got out the car and made my way into the house to cuddle with my man. When I got in the house, Troy was sitting in the living room watching *Don't Be a Menace in South Central While Drinking Your Juice in the Hood*. That was his favorite movie; he got a kick out of the shit.

I jumped on the couch and crawled over to him. We had a huge ass sectional in the living room that came with two big ass ottomans, and if you pushed them close to the couch you were able to put your feet up and relax.

"Hey Sunshine, how was your day?"

"Pretty good, you like my hair?" I asked while lying on his chest.

"Yea, I like it, but why you always wearing these weaves and shit when you have a head full of hair?"

"Because my hair is hard to manage unless I get a perm, and I don't want to perm my hair."

"So wear a 'fro." Troy said.

"I certainly will not do a such thing. How was your day?" I asked him.

"Umm, it was aight."

"That's it? Just aight? What did you do today?"

"Stash came over and we chopped it up a bit. Spoke to him about some shit."

"Some shit like what?" I asked curious.

"Just some shit that came to my attention a few days ago, I wasn't sure how to handle it."

"Oh okay." I said.

Troy then took a deep breath.

"Alright, check this Sunshine. I got some shit to tell you and I hope you take it well ma."

"Is it bad?"

"Kind of."

"Are you afraid of getting shot?" I asked picking at my big toe nail.

"Yes, so that's why that purse is staying down here and you're going to come upstairs with me."

I looked up at Troy who was now standing up.

"Ok, let's go."

I got up off the couch and followed him up the stairs. I got dizzy for a quick second.

"You alright?"

"Yea I'm ok, I think I got up too fast."

"What have you eaten today?"

"California Rolls."

"Again Sunshine? Yo' ass gonna turn into a roll, Rollie Pollie."

"Shut up, you're so whack."

We walked into his office and he motioned for me to sit on his lap.

"Read this baby."

I took the papers and started reading them. I had to read them twice to make sure I understood what was going on.

"Babe, you have a son. Aren't you excited?"

"Wait, you're not mad?"

"No, this was four years ago, why would I be mad?"

"You right, I don't know why I thought you would be on some petty shit. I'm sorry, ma."

"Sorry for what? When do you get him?"

"I guess whenever I have the time to go to Atlanta."

"Who is he staying with?"

"Foster family."

"Oh hell no! We'll catch a flight first thing tomorrow, he don't need to be in foster care when we has a home up here with us."

Troy just sat there shaking his head. "That's why I fucking love you girl. You never cease to amaze me. I appreciate this shit, for real Sunshine."

"Don't sweat it; I do want to know the back story with you and this Linda chick, but after my nap."

"Nap? Girl it's six o'clock, you ain't got time for a nap."

"Watch me. This is about us, we can arrive a little late to our engagement party."

Before I lay down, I texted Onyx and Sony to check on my prisoner and I sat my phone down and dozed off.

It felt like I was only sleep for fifteen minutes before Troy was shaking me to get up.

"Get up Sunshine, its 7:30."

"Ah shit!" I jumped up real fast and ran to take a shower. Troy had my dress already laid out when I got out, so all I had to do was lotion up and slip it on. I sprayed myself with perfume, took my silk bonnet off, and let my curls fall down. TaTa did her thing with that wand.

I grabbed my phone, my clutch and I didn't even bother putting on my shoes.

I ran down the stairs and Troy was waiting for me at the bottom, looking just as sexy as he wanted in his Armani Tux that Capri picked out for him. She knows her cousin too well because it fit him perfectly. Here I was worried about Troy shooting the club up for what I was wearing, but bitches better not even look his way for too long or I'm turning all the way up.

"Damn girl, if I hadn't already knocked you up, I would have definitely been doing that shit tonight. Daammnn, turn around for me."

I did as he asked.

"Capri got good taste."

"Yes she does, 'cause we both looking like a bucket of chicken wings at the Johnson's Family Reunion.

"You dumb girl. Come on, let's get up out of here."

We hopped in his new 2016 Acura NSX and were on our way to the club.

Chapter 24

Troy

When we pulled up to the club, there was a crowd of people. I couldn't even pull into the parking lot. I beeped the horn and the crowd split.

Damn, my cousin really went all out. I know my ass is going to have a heart attack when I look at that bank statement. There was a red carpet, I guess for me to drive down that led to the front door, a Marquee with bright lights that said the 'Congratulations to the future Mr. and Mrs. Jones', and there were velvet ropes, spotlights and photographers everywhere taking pictures. You would have thought we were Jay-Z and Beyoncé. I drove down the red carpet until the valet asked me to stop. I was about to go off 'cause this was my club I could do what I wanted, but I thought about it; it must have been a part of Capri's plan, so I went with it. He came over and opened my door for me to get out. He waved for my keys and I knew then this nigga had lost his mind.

"My car can stay right here. Don't nobody drive this here but me."

"Yes Mr. Jones," the valet said. I gave him a hundred-dollar tip and he backed off into the crowd.

I fixed my suit jacket and walked around to let my beautiful fiancée out.

She stepped out looking stunning, working that dress and her little baby bump. We walked the red carpet, stopping to take pictures. I must have really been feeling myself because I even stopped and posed like I was Tyson Beckford or some shit. There were people yelling and screaming "congratulations."

When we got down to the end of the red carpet, that's where our family was waiting. Even G-ma was there in her best dress.

"Look at you looking as good as you want to, G-ma." I reached over and gave her a hug.

"Aiight now, don't be trying to feel me up. I'm your grandmother."

"G-ma, ain't nobody trying to feel ya old ass up, do you see my wife to be?" I took Camilla's hand and had her spin around.

"That ain't got nothing on this," G-ma said putting her hands on her hips and doing a little spin for everybody. We all started laughing.

"You girl," I said pointing to Capri, "get over here." She walked to me and I hugged her.

"You really did your thing cuz. Can't wait to see what the wedding is going to look like."

"Aww, I'm happy you like it cousin, but wait until you see the inside."

"Oh, and I'm going to kick your ass for picking that dress out for Camilla; you must want to get somebody's head knocked off."

"Shut up, nigga and let's go inside, I need a drink. This planning shit is stressful."

Camilla

We walked inside club and I was floored. Everything was silver, glittery and shiny. Even the bartenders were wearing silver, glittered outfits. There was even a disco ball. There was a screen above the stage that had pictures of me and Troy flashing across it. She made the stage into a VIP section for our friends and family. It was really amazing how this girl pulled this off.

Capri finally let the crowd in and the night got started. I noticed all of the dancers were here except Onyx. His little horny ass was probably at the warehouse where he always was. He'll probably come later.

It was now 11:30pm; the party was supposed to be over at midnight.

Capri got up to the mic tipsy as ever, and demanded everyone's attention. The room got quiet.

"I would like to thank everyone for coming and for coming in peace. I appreciate y'all not tearing my cousin's shit up."

Yup she was done for the night.

"Now I'm going to let the guests of honor say a few words. Troy, Cami, come say a little somethin', somethin'," she said turning towards us.

I started laughing. "Baby, ya cousin is drunk. I think she had too many of them tongue twisters."

"Word," he laughed.

We went up and he grabbed the mic, said a little thank you speech to everyone for coming and a big thank you to the drunk in the back, referring to Capri.

I, too, got up and thanked everyone and hoped to see some of them at the wedding. As I was looking out in the crowd, I noticed a face that shouldn't have been there. She gave me a little smirk and ran off. I dropped the mic and ran back looking for my bag, and remembered I only came with this little ass clutch.

"Sunshine, you alright?" Troy asked.

"No, how the fuck did Keyonna get loose?"

"What? Where did you see Keyonna?"

"She was in the crowd Troy, smiling right at me."

He stood up and looked but she was long gone by then.

I pulled out my phone and I had eight missed calls, a voicemail, a text message and a picture message, all from Onyx.

I tried calling him back but it was going straight to voicemail. I opened the message and it said Keyonna wasn't there anymore; he was calling to see if I had moved her. That was at 7:30, right after I texted him.

I opened the picture message and my heart dropped.

It was a picture of Onyx lying on the floor of the warehouse bleeding from the head. I listened to the voicemail; it was Keyonna.

"Yea bitch, you thought you had me right. You made a mistake by not killing me, but I won't make that same mistake. Watch your back bitch."

I showed Troy the messages and he listened to voicemail. I saw his jaws tighten and I knew he was mad.

Just as he was handing me back the phone, all hell broke loose.

Troy

After listening to Keyonna's voice on Camilla's phone, I was mad as hell. I told Camilla to hurry up and deal with her. She had no idea the pull this bitch's father had.

Just as I was handing Camilla back her phone, gunshots rang out. I grabbed Camilla bringing her to ground. The shooting stopped and I looked over in VIP because I heard screaming. Stash had everyone down on the ground already. I was trying to figure out which one of my people was doing the screaming and if they were hit; it was TaTa. The gunshots had stopped so I pulled Camilla up and took her over to the VIP section where everyone else was. I went to check on Tata and she seemed to be ok; she was doing all that screaming for no reason, just being dramatic like always. I shook my head at that fool.

Stash and I gathered everyone up and we all ran to the back. The crowd was already making their way out the door.

Then the windows came shattering and we heard shots from an AK-47. I pushed Camilla on to the elevator and Stash scurried everyone else into the elevator. I gave Camilla my key.

"All of you are to stay upstairs until I come back."

"Where the hell you going Troy? I'm coming with you."

"No you're not, Camilla. You're pregnant, stay with your mom."

I looked over everyone's faces to make sure everyone was good. Fucking TaTa was the only one crying like a little bitch. I looked over to Kitty and I thought I saw a smirk on her face. I gave her an *I got my eyes on you* look and used the key to close the elevator door.

"You got heat?" Stash asked.

"Always," I said reaching behind me to get my gun and I felt a stinging pain. I didn't even realize I got shot in the shoulder.

Stash and I stayed downstairs to make sure nobody came into the club. We walked over to the entrance of the empty club to look out. There was no one, just my car sitting there.

"When people hear gunshots they clear out quickly," Stash said.

I laughed, "For real dog."

"What's this shit about man?" he asked.

I ran down the story about Camilla kidnapping Keyonna, Stan sending me a message and how Keyonna escaped, Onyx being dead and Camilla spotting Keyonna in the crowd before shots were fired.

As we were walking back to the elevator, I heard a big ass explosion. I prayed it wasn't what I thought it was. I walked back to the entrance and it was exactly that.

Fuck man, 155,000 dollars down the drain.

Camilla

I couldn't believe this shit was happening. How the fuck did this bitch get away? If only I had waited for Onyx text before my ass took a nap, this shit could have been avoided. I can't wait to catch that bitch again; I was definitely killing that bitch on the spot. I looked over at our family and they were all just sitting there. My mom and Tata were the only ones who looked scared.

I looked over to G-Ma, Ma and Ms. Viv and they were cooling like they see this shit every day. Troy's family really was some gangsters. The funniest thing was seeing G-ma rolling a blunt in the corner.

"Old woman, put that away. You are definitely not about to smoke that around me," I said pointing to my pregnant belly.

I guess gunshots sober a person up quick cause Pri's ass was pacing back and forth looking like she was ready for war. I guess she was just as worried about Stash as I was for Troy.

Kitty on the other hand, was just sitting there picking her nails.

"Kitty you alright, mama?"

"Yea I'm okay; I just hope Troy and Stash are okay."

I didn't believe her.

I reached under Troy's desk and turned on the cameras that covered the whole club. I flicked through the screens and found Troy and Stash; they were okay. I flipped through the screens again in search of anyone else in the building. The building was empty. I switched screens to outside just in time to see Troy's brand new car go up in flames.

"Damn, 155, 000 down the fucking drain," I said.

I know Troy is pissed.

Troy

After ensuring the cost was clear, we loaded everyone up and got them home safely. Being that Stash and I didn't live too far from each other, Camilla and I jumped in the car with them.

"Y'all get home safe alright, let me know when y'all get home."

"Alright," said a now sober Capri.

"Thanks again cuz, I really appreciate what you did. Let me know when you want to get that interior decorating business off the floor. You got my vote."

"Ok… sorry it was ruined. For the wedding, I promise to look for a bulletproof building and have heavy security."

I started laughing. "Nah, you ain't got to worry about that. Whoever did this will be dealt with by the time the wedding comes."

"Ok. Bye Cami," she reached out and gave her hug.

"Y'all get home safe, ok," Camilla said to them.

We waved bye to them and walked into the house.

I watched as Camilla sat down on the couch. She looked to be in a lot of pain, probably from when I pulled her to the ground.

"You ok baby?"

"No, I want to kill that bitch and everyone involved."

"I ain't talking about that, I don't care about that shit. I'm talking about you and the baby."

"Oh, we're okay. Sorry, that I got us into this shit. I know this was the wrong time to be starting a war. I wish I had known I was pregnant before I kidnapped Keyonna; I probably would have thought twice before risking our lives."

"Nah, don't worry about that. Stan was threatening to get at me way before you kidnapped Keyonna. That was just a little fuel to an already lit fire. I'll handle Stan's fat ass." She kicked her shoes off and laid her head on my lap.

"Can I keep it real with you, ma?"

"Don't you always?"

"Yea I do. I think Kitty had something to do with this."

"Why would you think that?"

"When everyone got on the elevator I thought I saw a smirk on her face like she was enjoying the shit that was happening."

"Now that you mentioned it, I did overhear a conversation that she was having earlier when we were getting our hair done. She was telling someone to be there on time and not to fuck up her plan.

Do you think this was her plan? And she and Keyonna are working together?"

"Maybe, but what's her reason behind turning against us?"

"I don't know baby, but I'm damn sure going to find out."

"Nah, stay away from her Sunshine. I don't need you putting yourself at risk by falling into one of her traps."

"Ok," Camilla said but it wasn't convincing enough. I sat her up.

"Sunshine, I mean it. It's not just you anymore. You're carrying our child, you have to be careful."

"Ok," she said.

"Are you still down for Atlanta tomorrow?" Troy asked.

"Yea, I want to meet little man. Are you upset about your car?" I asked Troy.

"Nah, I'll have Donny put in an offer for the other one that's somewhere out in the world." Troy said.

She let out a laugh before I heard her snore. I laughed because she swears up and down she doesn't snore.

Camilla

We woke up the next morning, packed a light bag and jumped in the Range, making our way to Newark airport to catch a flight to Atlanta. I brought my laptop and my books so that I could finish my paper for class. Troy laid back and took a nap. I put in my earphones and started going in on my paper.

Two hours later, the plane was landing. I don't know why I was expecting to be on the plane for at least four hours. I woke Troy up to let him know we were there.

We got walked through the terminal and went outside to look for a taxi. Troy was able to hail one and it took us to our hotel.

Troy got us a presidential suite for the weekend. I started making some phone calls to the lawyer and to the foster agency. I was finally able to get in touch with the foster agency and they said they needed to hear from the lawyer before they released the boy to us. I called the lawyer until he finally picked up. We set up a meeting for tomorrow at ten o'clock in the morning.

I let Troy know everything. Being that we had a whole day to waste, we went out and enjoyed ATL. I had never been, but Troy has so he was pretty familiar with the place. We went to Enterprise and got a rental so that we were able to get around. By the end of the night, we ended up at a soul food restaurant in downtown Atlanta because I had a taste for some collard greens, baked mac and cheese, candied yams and oxtails. Once we were done eating, I was ready to go to bed, and that we did.

The next morning we woke up at nine o'clock, ate breakfast and went to see a man about a little boy.

Troy

I was nervous as hell to meet a four year old. I guess I just hoped I was everything he would need in a father. I was new to this so I didn't know how to act. Yesterday when Camilla and I were out, I picked up a football for him. I didn't know what else to get him.

We decided to meet at a park not too far from the hotel. We pulled into the parking lot of the park and my hands were sweating.

"It's ok baby, he'll love you."

"I hope so."

We got out the car and walked to the bench where I saw a black man in a suit, a white couple and the little boy I recognized from the picture, playing with a toy car. I didn't even know his name.

I got closer and was greeted by the lawyer.

"Hello, I'm Troy Jones, and this here is my fiancée, Camilla Baxter.

"Hello, I'm Linda's, well *was* Linda's lawyer, Brian Powell. This here is Mr. and Mrs. Turner and this here," he said walking over to the kid who didn't even bother to look up. "This is Malachi." He then looked up and smiled at me. That was when it was confirmed that this was my boy. He had my smile and my muscular face; shit, he looked just like me.

I walked over to him and introduced myself. Before I could say anything he said, "You're my dad."

"Yes little man, I am. How did you know?"

"My mom showed me a picture."

He jumped down from the table and went over to his suitcase and pulled out a picture of me at the grand opening of my club. She had to pull this from the club's Facebook page.

I was happy that he already knew who I was. I didn't have to do too much. I introduced him to Camilla and he looked up and asked if she was going to be his new mommy. She teared up a little and told him yes she was. She asked him if he wanted to come live with us and he shook his head up and down, while still playing with his car.

We signed all the legal papers that needed to be signed to get custody of Malachi, before Mr. Powell and the Turners left.

We stayed at the park for a little while, while he played with Camilla on the slide and swings.

When they were done, we left and went to get food and headed back to the hotel room; we were leaving tomorrow morning. I had Camilla order Malachi a ticket because we already had ours. When we got back to the hotel room, Camilla pulled out the sofa bed and made the bed for him to sleep. That reminded me I had nothing for him—no bed, no clothes, toys, nothing. I had to find him a school to go to and schedule him a doctor's visit. Thank God for Camilla because she was willing to do it all.

I didn't even tell my mother about me having a son. I know she's going to be mad I didn't tell her, but excited to have him as a part of the family.

The next morning we woke up and packed all of our clothes and got up out of there. Malachi had never been on a plane, so he was a bit scared as to be expected. He cried himself to sleep and I prayed he slept for the next two hours, and that he did.

When we arrived back to Newark, we collected our luggage and hopped in the car and were on our way home. It was three o'clock in the afternoon when we arrived home. Malachi was amazed by the house. He started running throughout the house, up the stairs, down the patio stairs, he even wanted to get in the pool but he had no trunks. I took him upstairs so that he could pick out which bedroom he wanted. Before we got on the plane in Atlanta, I told G-ma I had a surprise for everyone and that I wanted her to have Sunday dinner at her house tonight. I needed to take little man out to get some new clothes and toys and maybe stop at Ikea to see if they had furniture for a little boy. I was excited and nervous at the same time to be a dad. Now that my son was in the picture, I knew I had to take Stan's ass down for real. I couldn't risk having him, Camilla and our unborn child at risk. I think I let it go on too long without addressing it, and it blew up in my face at the engagement party.

We went to Willowbrook Mall to shop for Malachi. I really wanted to go to Garden State, but it was Sunday and Bergen County didn't sell clothes on Sunday. We went to the Gap and Old Navy and Camilla pick him out everything he would need apparel wise. We went to Foot Locker and I got him a couple pairs of sneakers. We took him to Toys R US and he went bananas. I ended up spending the most in there. After we were done, we drove over to Ikea out in Elizabeth to check out some furniture. We picked out a reversible bed for him and we got the royal blue dresser and chest to match the lime green and blue bed in the bag. We purchased a lime green shag carpet to go in the middle of the room. By the time we were done spending on this kid, I had to spend at least five thousand on him. I didn't mind; this made up for the four years I missed of his life. I didn't even know when his birthday was. I had to read those papers again.

By the time we were done shopping, it was about seven o'clock in the evening. Ikea was going to have the furniture delivered tomorrow. We had Malachi change out of his dingy look clothes he had on and put on something new I had just brought him. I thought it would be cute if he and I matched, so I went and put on the exact same thing, my black jeans, a white t and my black and white new Retro 9 Jordan's.

I was downstairs brushing little man's hair and Camilla came downstairs.

"Awww don't y 'all look cute."

"No, I look cute, Daddy copied me."

We started laughing. "Yes baby, you look cute and Daddy is a copycat."

"Shut up little nappy head," I said grabbing the top of his head and shaking it. Little man, when is your birthday?

"April 5, 2011."

"Ayyyeee," Camilla yelled, "that's my birthday, too, give me five!"

We all left out the house and made our way to G-ma's house. We got there and everyone seemed to be there. I had Camilla stay in the car until I signaled for her to come in. I walked into the house and said hi to everyone. Like always, I got cursed out by G-ma for being late. I got everyone into the living room and I got everyone's attention and told them I had a surprise for them. I walked outside and signaled for Camilla to come in with Malachi. They walked into the house and I let Camilla go in first and say hi to everyone. I walked in with Malachi behind me.

"Everyone, I want y'all to meet Malachi." He came from behind me and I heard my mother gasp for air. G-ma just stared at him.

"This is my son. He's been living in Atlanta for the last four years. I knew nothing about him. The only reason I found out about him was because his mother, Linda, died recently from a brain aneurysm. I received legal papers last week stating that he was mine and if I didn't take custody of him he would end up in foster care permanently. That's why Camilla and I went down to Atlanta this weekend.

My mother got up and walked over to him. She had tears in her eyes.

"Oh my God, Troy, he looks just like you when you were younger. He's a spitting image of you. Hi Malachi, I'm your grandma. I'm your daddy's mommy. Can I have a hug?"

Malachi reached over and hugged my mom. Once they were done hugging, she walked him over to introduce him to everyone. He was a bit scared of G-ma, but by the end of the night he was getting a kick out of her.

He played himself to sleep, lying on Camilla's lap.

"So Cami, baby, how you feel about this whole thing?" my mother asked her.

"I'm perfectly fine with it, he calls me mommy," she said with a smile. "I wasn't ready to take on a mother role when I first found out I was pregnant, but having him around me really has me looking forward to this mothering thing."

We sat there a little longer until Camilla started to get tired. I promised my mother I would bring him to her tomorrow so that they could spend some time together.

The next morning, Camilla went and registered Malachi for pre-school and took him to the doctor. I stayed at home and waited for the furniture to come. They didn't come until one in the afternoon and I had them set the whole room up. So when little man came back, all he had to do was enjoy his new space. I was really getting the hang of this new fathering thing. I couldn't wait until we found out what Camilla was having so we could do the other room. Hopefully it was a girl. Camilla was now five months and Dr. McDaniel said we would be able to find out at our next visit. The wedding was in two weeks and Camilla wanted a getaway for two days. I was reluctant but I agreed to it.

Chapter 25

Kitty

I haven't heard from Camilla or Capri since the night of the engagement party. I wonder if they were on to me. The only way I was going to find out was to call one of them. I decided to call Camilla to see how she was doing…fake like I cared.

"Hey girl how you?"

"I'm okay Kitty, how you feeling?"

"I'm good… what happed the other night was crazy, huh?"

"Yea, it was."

"I wonder who that was shooting at us."

"I don't know, but Troy is looking into it. He's pretty pissed because his mother and grandmother were there. I feel bad for whoever was responsible."

"So what are you up to?"

"Nothing, on my way over to Capri's house. We're going out to the Hamptons so she can show me the wedding location."

"Oh really? Aww, I wanted to come."

"Hey Kitty, I'm going to call you back, Troy's on the other end."

I watched her hang up with me and put her phone down. Fucking liar, Troy wasn't on the other end. I was now convinced that they may have been on to me.

I've been following Camilla the whole day. She had some little boy with her this morning. I wonder who this kid was.

I watched her drop the kid off to Troy and I wrote the house address down. I forwarded the text message and I sat in the car and waited.

They didn't come out until about six o'clock. Camilla got in the car by herself and Troy and the boy got into another car together. Seeing them two side by side, it dawned on me that this had to be his son. I wonder what chick was lucky enough to carry Troy's firstborn son. They pulled off and I waited for Camilla to pull off, too. When she did, I followed behind her.

Troy

Malachi and I were on our way to my mom's house. Malachi was going to spend the night with my mom's so I could handle some business.

My mom was at the shop so that's where I was dropping him off. Soon as we walked in, he ran straight to my mom. The ladies and Tata ate him up. He was a charmer just like his dad. Once again, I wanted to do the daddy/son matching thing. I though the shit was cute. He fell in love with Red. I think it was because she had a fat ass, in which I agreed.

I looked over Kayla's chair and her space was empty.

"What happened to that chicken head?"

"I don't know, she just up and quit the other day."

"Thank God, because I don't need my pregnant daughter-in-law coming up in here and having to beat a thot down again." Everybody laughed.

"Ma, stop saying thot, do you even know what a thot is?"

"Yup, that hoe over there was a thot." This time I laughed with everybody.

"Y 'all need to stop teaching my mother how to be ratchet. I know it's yo ass, Tata."

"Un-uh, it ain't me Troy," she said grabbing her chest. "I'm not ratchet. I'm a classy lady."

"Yea, whatever. Not the way yo' ratchet ass was screaming the other night."

"For real bitch, was all that necessary?" Red asked.

"My life was in jeopardy; sorry, I don't get shot at on regular basis. And I was drinking and liquor makes me a little dramatic."

I shook my head and laughed. She was funny. Although she gets on my nerve, if anybody fucked with Tata they had to see me first. She's been around a long time. Her family abandoned her a long time ago because they couldn't accept her lifestyle. I thought it was fucked up. My mom took her in and became like a mother to her.

"Alright y'all, I'll catch y'all later. Take care of my little man, alright?"

"Bye Troy," all the ladies said at once.

I left out.

I called Stash and told him to meet me at club. I had plans to handle Stan's fat ass today. That's why I was okay with Camilla going out of town and Malachi staying at my mom's.

Stash met me at the club and we went up to my office. I walked over to a wall that I had custom built where I hid my arsenal of guns. I had every gun that was ever made. Stash brought Big Shirley and her sister Big Bertha. I knew Stan's house like the back of my hand. After grabbing a few guns and some bullets, we put on our bulletproof vests; although I didn't plan on getting shot at, it was still safe to have them on. We made our way out the door.

"So where we going?"

"Stan's house is surrounded by trees. You can pick anyone of those trees and start picking off the guards. I want Stan to myself."

Although I could have handled all of them by myself, I didn't want to alert Stan and have him getting away on me.

"Alright dog, just give me the signal to start peeling off."

"Alright."

We pulled up around the block from Stan's house and got out. Stash went one way I went the other. I got low in the bushes. I gave Stash the ok to start getting at them. He knocked the guard that circles the building, off first. Soon as he did that, I ran to the house and climbed the drain pipe that was on the side of the house. I shimmied up the pipe and on to the balcony that led to Stan's office. I peeked inside and the fat fuck was inside talking to his right-hand,

Javier. I kicked in the door and started spraying bullets. I caught Javier in the stomach and he went down. Stan had started fumbling looking for his gun.

It was funny because when he realized he couldn't get to his gun, he started trying to crawl away from me.

Fucking pathetic.

"What was all that shit you were talking nigga, huh?"

"Fuck you Troy and that bitch of yours. You fucked with my baby girl, so I fucked with your family."

"Well guess what? You're going to be meeting your baby where you're going 'cause I'm sending her ass too," I said before letting my gun blast sending one to the dome.

I left out the same way I came in. I climbed down the drain and Stash met me at the bottom.

"It's done bro?"

"Yea, I told you it wasn't going to be an issue handling Stan."

We walked back to the car, hopped in and pulled off.

Camilla

Pri and I were sitting at her house chilling and drinking wine.

Well I had a glass and this lush put the straw in the bottle and finished off the rest of the bottle. We sat there talking all night. Pri opened up to me about her two miscarriages she had, and how she was scared to try again because she didn't want to get Stash's hopes up just to let him down again.

It was going on midnight when we decided to take it down. Pri was tipsy from the wine, so she hugged me and walked up the stairs to go to bed. I was staying in the guest room on the first floor. I decided to call Troy to see what he was doing. I walked into the kitchen to look for some cookies, cake or something. This baby had me starving like Marvin.

Kitty

I was posted outside of Capri's house for a few hours. I grabbed my gun and got out. I snuck around the back of the house, and climbed over the gate to the backyard. I walked up the stairs to the door of the master bedroom. I looked in the window and saw Capri lying in the bed. I put the silencer on and twisted the knob to the door. It was locked. Good thing I made sure to grab a credit card before I got out the car. I jiggled the card and the lock popped. I put the card in my back pocket and walked in. Capri was sleep. I aimed the gun at her head and fired, sending a bullet to her head.

One down one to go.

I walked down the stairs and I heard Camilla's voice, but I wasn't sure which room it was coming from. I got further down the stairs and I heard moving in kitchen. I walked toward the kitchen and Camilla was sitting at the island with her back towards me. I aimed my gun at her.

Bet this bitch ain't see this shit coming.

"This is for Supreme!"

Boom… Boom…

Troy

I got home and was ready to take it down. I called my mom to check on Malachi and she said he was asleep. As I was hanging up with my mother, my phone rung and it was Camilla. I sat on the phone with her for a minute; she was complaining about the baby making her eat so much she was going to need a mommy makeover after she pushed her out.

"Shut up with that shit, you'll be fine, and if you do gain a little I'll be right there in the gym with you Sunshine."

"I love you, Troy."

"I love you, Sunshine,"

I heard what sounded like a gun cock and Kitty's voice say, "this is for Supreme" and two gun shots.

"Camilla!" I yelled into the phone.

Nothing.

"Camilla!" I yelled again.

I could hear her gasping for breath.

Shit! I dropped the phone and rushed out the door. I was stopped in my tracks by a gun pointed to my chest.

"This is for my father."

Fuck!

BOOM!

To be continued.........

Text ROYALTY to 42828 to keep up with our new releases!

Looking for a publishing home?

Royalty Publishing House, Where the Royals reside, is accepting submissions for writers in the urban fiction genre. If you're interested, submit the first 3-4 chapters with your synopsis to submissions@royaltypublishinghouse.com. Check out our website for more information: www.royaltypublishinghouse.com.

Be sure to LIKE our Royalty Publishing House
page on Facebook

CPSIA information can be obtained
at www.ICGtesting.com
Printed in the USA
LVOW10s1732190118
563158LV00012B/860/P

9 781517 725426